WHEN LUCK
RUNS OUT

WHEN LUCK RUNS OUT

BY TERRI KARSTEN

WAGONBRIDGE PUBLISHING

First Edition, paperback
ISBN: 978-0-9962863-3-6

This novel is a work of historical fiction. While care has been
taken to provide a historically accurate background for the work,
the characters, events, and locations presented within are the
products of the author's imagination or have been used to create
a fictitious story.

Wagonbridge Publishing
661 East Howard St.
Winona, MN 55987

For Brandon, Keary and Rory,
who grew up with Meg and Mole

With heartfelt thanks to the multitude of readers, critiquers, research librarians and archivists who have helped make this book better. Poor Meg and Mole might still be sitting on the shelf without your generous help.

This book was made possible, in part, by a work-in-progress grant from the Society of Children's Book Writers and Illustrators.

CHAPTER 1: HOME, SUCH AS IT IS

The sun was setting as Meg trudged home along Cherry Street. She hunched against the jostling crowd of hawkers and peddlers. A gust of wind swept past her, rattling bits of trash against an iron fence and carrying the faint odor of roasting corn from some happier part of the city.

Just ahead, a rag picker stopped his cart to fix a broken harness strap. Horse drawn buses and buggies piled up behind him, but Meg paid scant attention to the curses of the angry drivers. She took the chance to dash across the street in front of the rag picker's cart, and turned into the alley that led to the room she shared with Ma and her brother.

The alley, unpaved and muddy from yesterday's rain, was quiet after Cherry Street, but not empty. Grimy men crouched beside trash heap fires and a gang of teenage boys pitched pennies by a stoop. A string of younger children played crack the whip.

Meg ignored them all, plodding slowly homeward, until the tail end of the children's line swung into her with a noisy flurry. She jumped back, landing in a puddle. Water seeped into her boots. Meg swore and shook a fist at them. The children scattered out of her way, but Meg was too tired to chase them.

Hurrying now, she walked past the clapboard tenement houses. These wooden buildings were six stories high and leaned against each other, as if they might fall down without the support of a neighbor. Each building was crammed full of poor immigrant families crowding into New York. Meg lived in the fourth house in the row. She climbed the stone steps and started to push open the door.

A small voice from the corner stopped her. "Hey, Meg."

"Mole?" Meg hooked her snarled red-brown hair behind her ears to peer at the ragged little boy crouched in the shadows. The gas lights shining on Cherry Street were too dim to reach into the alleys, but she knew her brother. "What are you doing out? It's getting late."

Mole shrugged. "Ma's not home yet. Jake's there."

Meg's stomach churned angrily as it always did when she thought of Jake. Nevertheless, she reached for her brother's hand.

He pulled back from her. "Don't let's go in yet, Meg. Look here. See what I caught?" He held up a big, black beetle.

Meg made a face. "Ugh. Ma will have a fit." Meg knew Ma wouldn't really notice, but it was no use thinking that way. "Get rid of it and come along. You can't stay here without a jacket. It's going to rain again tonight."

Mole slipped the beetle into his pocket.

Meg pushed him inside, letting the rough wood door bang shut behind them. She didn't blame Mole for wanting to stay outside, but like it or not, home was inside.

Stale air closed in on Meg like a coffin. She paused for her eyes to adjust to the dark. Here and there a bit of light spilled out under a door or through a crack in the wall, but there were no lamps in the hallway. Mole skittered on ahead. He didn't mind the rats.

They passed all the way through the front building and through another door to the rear house, tacked on the back. The front part of the tenement was rickety, but the rear house was even worse. Here the floor creaked and wobbled under their feet. The walls, blackened with soot and dirt, smelled of stale urine and old sweat. Meg wrinkled her nose. She hated the smell most of all. She followed Mole up the stairs.

At the third floor Mole slowed and dawdled behind her. Their room was to the left of the stairs. Meg knocked and tried the door. Often it was locked against them, but not tonight. They slipped quietly inside.

The room was small, without any windows. An oil lamp on the

table gave a smoky light. Mole crawled onto the bed on one side of the door. Up and down the hallway, on each of the six floors, families filled such rooms, often a dozen or more people in one tiny room. Meg guessed she ought to feel grateful her family was so small, only Ma and Mole and herself.

And now Jake.

"It's about time you got here," Jake said. He straddled the only chair in the room. His face was stubbly from not shaving and the jagged scar on his forehead was pink against his dirty skin. Jake wasn't family at all, only Ma's boyfriend. "How much did you get today?" His breath smelled of beer.

Meg scowled and stuck up her chin. "It's my money. Mine and Ma's." Unwilling to turn her back on him, she sidled past to the other side of the table and set her apple bag on the shelf.

"None of your lip!" Jake half rose out of the chair. "I've had about all I can take of you and that weasly brother of yours!"

Meg cringed away from him. 'Then get out of here,' she thought, but didn't have the courage to say out loud. Gripping the edge of the table to keep her hands from trembling, she narrowed her eyes and pressed her lips together tightly.

"I'll whip that sass outta you!" Jake raised his arm to hit her.

Meg braced herself. It wouldn't be the first time. He never hit them when Ma was home, only when she was late, like tonight.

Just then a rattle at the door took Jake's attention. Ma came in and caught Jake's arm. "Leave her be, darlin'." Even after years in America, Ma's voice still carried a heavy Irish brogue. "She's none of your lookout." Ma turned to Meg and held out her hand. "You'll be giving me the day's money."

Meg reached into her skirt pocket and dug out the handful of coins she had earned today. Reluctantly, she dropped them into Ma's outstretched hand.

Ma counted the coins. She smiled to herself. Then without looking at Meg, she handed the money to Jake and took off her shawl.

"Ma!" Meg snatched for the coins, but Jake held them out of reach. "Don't..."

"You shush," Ma interrupted. Wisps of hair hung in her face, but she made no move to brush it aside. She kissed Jake in a way that made Meg grit her teeth in helpless rage.

Jake tossed a coin in the air and caught it. "Here, boy," he called to Mole. "Fetch me a growler of beer." Mole slid reluctantly off the bunk, looking at Ma and then Meg, but not Jake.

"Leave the boy out of it, darlin'. You know I'm not after him hanging by the pub, not yet." Ma held Jake's right hand, the mangled one, and let her fingers play along his arm. She laughed gaily, a sound that used to make Meg smile, but not now, when it was always for Jake, and never for her or Mole. "You can be getting your own beer tonight."

Jake caught her hand and pulled her close to kiss her again. "Come on out with me. We'll have a gay time, dancing and drinking."

"And what have we to dance about?" Ma asked, but her sharp words were softened by her laughter. "Go ahead, darlin'. I'll just settle the bairns and catch up to you."

Jake gave her another kiss and winked at Meg, as if to prove he'd won again. Pulling his cap on with his good left hand, he went out.

"That was to go for the rent, Ma," Meg said as soon as the door closed. "Why did you give it to him?"

"Rent's not due for three days yet." Ma's smile was gone. "He's got a card game tonight. Maybe he'll help pay the rent."

"That's just a dream, Ma, and you know it. He's not paid once in the six months since the accident hurt his hand and put him out of work. What if we get turned out?"

"Don't you worry." Ma shook her head as if to clear the fog from it. "I get paid at the factory come Friday. That'll do."

"But Ma..."

"Hush your nagging." Ma ran her blue dye-stained hands through her tangled hair.

Meg looked up, matching Ma's stubborn anger.

Ma looked away first. "And don't be looking at me like that. Ain't I got enough trouble in this world without me own daughter to stare me down?"

Meg bit her lip to hold in her sharp words. She never meant to hurt Ma. But what were they going to eat, come Friday?

"Bring me the bottle, Mole." Ma beckoned impatiently.

Mole slid off the bed. He crawled underneath it to fetch the bottle of whiskey, hidden where Jake wouldn't find it.

"Don't, Mole." Meg frowned.

Mole stood up with the bottle in hand. He hesitated, shifting his eyes from his mother to his sister and back again.

"Come up here beside me, Moley." Ma patted the bare mattress.

Mole shrugged his bony shoulders in apology at Meg. Then he handed the bottle to Ma. She wrapped an arm around him and took a swig.

Meg folded her arms across her chest. Time was, Ma had wrapped an arm around her, but that time was long gone.

"You ought to kick him out," she said, half to herself. "Da would never have left us to go hungry."

Ma laughed bitterly. She took another swallow and wiped her mouth on her sleeve. "Do you see Da here now? Where's all the lovely food he'll be bringing us? Not here, you can be sure, and not like to be here. No, he's gone for good and well you know it."

"But you sent him away!" Meg said, the words bursting out before she could think. "You told him not to come back." The awful memory was as fresh as if it had been last night instead of six years ago.

Ma jumped up, knocking Mole over. "Shut up, girl!" she screamed. "Just you shut up! Da made his own choice, same as the rest of us. He deserted us, and there's no denying it." For a moment she glared at Meg through bloodshot eyes.

Then she crumpled and sat on the bed beside Mole. She sniffed loudly and blinked back tears of self-pity. "And me carrying the child," she mourned, squeezing Mole to her side. She turned a hard face to Meg. "He walked out on us, girl. Make no mistake about it."

Meg thought back to the night in June, 1863 when Da had left, a night she could not forget, no matter how she tried. They had lived in the front part of the tenement then and had a window. She had been sleeping on the fire escape because it was so hot, when her parents' angry voices had wakened her.

"Don't go, Mike," Ma said.

"I've got to, Ida. You know President Lincoln has called for the draft. I didn't cross the ocean to fight in anyone's war. Did you want to see me a soldier?"

Meg could see him through the window, pacing the floor. His wild hair, so like her own, made him look like a huge, shaggy dog. Meg had wanted to shout, "Don't go away, Da!" But she lay very still on her thin blanket, shivering in spite of the heat.

Ma had started crying. Da put his strong arm around her. She lay her head on his chest for only a minute, then pushed him away. "What about us?" she asked. "We need you. I've got a bad feeling about tonight. Stay home just the night, Mike. I'm begging you."

"I've got to go," Da repeated, "or else I'll be sent off to war."

"Then don't be coming back!" Ma screamed, pounding her fist on his chest.

Da stomped out, slamming the door. Meg crawled inside and squeezed up close to Ma, but Ma's arms were wrapped tightly around herself and not around Meg.

Da had not come back, not alive. His mates brought his body the next day. Ma had watched, dry-eyed and silent.

Meg had always believed it was Ma that killed him. Not the draft riots protesting the Civil War. Not the New York police he had been fighting. Ma could have stopped him. Meg had been too little. Ma should have.

Meg clenched her hands, then slowly unclenched them, and shook her head to clear away the thoughts of Da. Remembering him never helped keep Ma at home.

Ma swallowed, then stood up, handing Mole the bottle. "Meg, see to supper for you and the boy. I'll be back late."

"But Ma, you were out last night, and the night before. Can't you just stay tonight?"

Ma laughed, not the gay laughter she had used with Jake, but a sound filled with bitterness. "Stay here? And for what? To listen to you rant against me, your own mother? Don't be shaming me with your eyes, girl. I've a right to a little fun come evening. Lord knows I work hard the day long." She bent to kiss the top of Mole's head, then pushed him away. "Take care of your brother now and leave your poor ma alone."

"Don't I do that the day long?" Meg snapped. "It's his Ma he's needing now."

Ma whirled to slap her, but Meg ducked. Ma pulled the shawl around her shoulders and jerked open the door. "You got no call to judge me, girl, and no right to speak so against your own mother. You best be glad your da isn't here to see what shamelessness you've come to."

"And you're glad of it too, Ma, for your own shame," Meg screeched as Ma slammed the door behind her. "Jake is not Da, and he never will be."

In the silence that followed, Mole pulled on Meg's sleeve. "I'm hungry, Meg."

Meg ruffled his sandy hair absently, still smoldering. Ma never listened to her.

Mole pulled on her sleeve again. His pale, freckled face was smudged. Meg swiped at his face with her apron and gave him the last apple from her sack. "Work on this, while I fix us some supper." She brushed a hand across her eyes, trying to rub away the tiredness, but it was no use. She was always tired.

There were four potatoes left in the cupboard. Meg picked out three to put on the coals to roast. One for each of them. Except Jake. She'd die before she cooked for Jake, coming in a stranger and thinking he could take Da's place. Never! But she could do a kindness for Ma. Meg cut a couple of thick slices of bread from the hard loaf on the table.

Mole finished his apple, core and all. Then he sat on the floor with a small cardboard box. He put the big, black beetle he had caught in it.

"Didn't I tell you to get rid of that thing?" Meg said.

"He might get lost." Mole stroked the beetle's back with the tip of his finger, then closed the lid of the box.

"Fancy worrying over a beetle. Did you spend all day hunting that?" Meg asked sourly. "Couldn't you pick rags or black boots or do something useful? I was, time I was your age."

Mole didn't answer. He hunched up his shoulders and played with a piece of string he called a cockroach trap.

When the potatoes were done, Meg set them on the table.

Mole gobbled up his share before Meg was even half finished. "Isn't there any more?"

Meg looked at the hot potato waiting for Ma. She wouldn't come home until very late; too late to eat. It was a shame to waste a good, hot potato. "Go on." She shoved it toward Mole. "Ma probably won't be hungry tonight."

Meg blew out the lamp and crawled into bed beside Mole, but she lay awake for hours. When, finally, a key rattled in the lock and the door creaked open, she lay perfectly still.

Ma and Jake giggled and hushed each other with exaggerated whispers. Jake stumbled into the table, cursed, and knocked over the oil lamp when he tried to light it. The glass cracked against the wood table but didn't shatter.

Ma put her finger to his lips and shushed him. She set the lamp back up and struck a match to light it while Jake rummaged through the cupboard, looking for food. He tore at the last of the bread Meg had been saving for breakfast. Ma reached for a chunk, and he playfully held it out of her reach, until they both fell, laughing, on the bed.

Meg waited until Jake's coarse wheezing joined with Ma's gently ragged snores. Then she got up, tiptoed across the room and blew out the lamp. Only then did she slip back into bed and sleep.

CHAPTER 2: WITH NEVER A KIND WORD

Early the next morning Meg got up and dressed quietly, without lighting the lamp.

Ma woke anyway. "Are you up and off, thinking of leaving the boy alone today?"

"No, Ma. Don't I always take him with me? For all the good it does, since he runs off soon as my back is turned."

Ma sat up, shrugging her shoulders to ease the stiffness. "Sure I know. Just see he gets a good meal. That's little enough to ask, I'm thinking."

Meg thumped her fist on the table. "And how am I to do that? You let Jake use the money I had for beer."

Ma cradled her head in her hands as if Meg's fist had hit her instead of the table. "Ach, shush, girl. You'll be waking everyone."

Meg glared. Why should she care if she woke Jake? Still, she lowered her voice. "There's not a bit of bread left here. What am I to feed him then?"

"You'll have the apples, and once you sell a few, you can buy the bread."

"We could all do with some meat, Ma, or a hot pasty. We could have had that, if you hadn't gone off with Jake last night. He's ruining all of us, Ma. We don't need him."

Ma lay back on the bed. "Still harping on the same tune, though it be an old one by now." She gave an exaggerated sigh. "Sure, you're a selfish thing, with never a thought for me or your brother. Grudging me even the pleasure of one night. Be off with you then, if you've nothing but blame and never a kind word for your poor Ma. Never you fear. The day will come you'll be the sorrier for it."

Meg snatched her brown shawl off the chair and pulled roughly on Mole, who still lay sprawled on the bed. "Come on, Mole," she snapped. "Since we're neither of us wanted here."

Mole sat up sleepily.

Roughly, Meg pulled him off the bed and shoved his jacket at him. Ma always turned her thoughts around. It was no use trying to explain to her they needed more than bread.

"Don't worry none about us," she said over her shoulder to Ma, who had turned her back. Meg was too angry to care anymore if her words hurt. "Go ahead and drink and dance the night away without a care for your own children." Meg dragged Mole out the door, slamming it behind her and shutting out the sounds of Ma's crying.

Mole, still half dazed with sleep, stumbled after her. "Wait, Meg. Ma's crying. Oughtn't we go back and see to her?"

For an answer, Meg just pulled him faster along. She didn't speak until they were outside. Then it was only to order him to put his jacket on. She wrapped her shawl around her shoulders. The morning sun shone clear and bright, but a nip in the air made her shiver.

"Aw, Meg, do I have to?" Mole whined. "It's too small. I'm not cold."

"Just do what I tell you for once." She jerked on the front of the worn jacket to help him. He was right. The sleeves came halfway up to his elbows, and he couldn't get it buttoned.

"You want something better, you go rag-picking yourself." She sat down on the doorstep to put on her boots. She had bought them six months earlier at the second hand store with her own money. They really fit and were still shiny black in some places. She rubbed soot on them to hide the scuff marks.

"Mole needs boots too," Ma had said when she brought them home. "Can't you think of nobody but yourself?"

Meg scowled, remembering. So what if he needed boots? It wasn't her problem, was it? Still, he wouldn't be able to go barefoot much longer. Winter would be here soon. She chewed the tangled ends of her hair. It would take the winter to save enough for another pair of boots, and that only if she could keep the money from Jake.

It hadn't always been this way. They were poor, Meg knew, even before Da died. But not like this. They had food then and shoes to wear. Even more, there had been laughter. Now there was only bitter words and fighting.

When had the laughter died? Meg tried to remember. When Mole was born? When they had left the first apartment and moved to the rear house? Or when Ma met Jake and invited him in?

"Come on, Meg, let's go." Mole tugged at her sleeve, impatient now that he was awake.

She took his hand as they walked down the alley.

"Can we eat?" Mole asked suddenly.

"Later. We'll get apples first."

They walked past closed shops and rows of silent tenement houses. In the pale light of dawn, the buildings loomed over the street like sleeping giants. Gradually, newsboys, peddlers, and factory workers began filling up the streets. Meg didn't stop to talk to anyone.

With Mole skipping ahead, as familiar with the way as she was, they came to a large warehouse by the docks and went around to a side door. Five girls milled about.

Meg slipped in among them without a word. As they waited, more girls joined the crowd, pushing to get to the front of the line. Meg elbowed them out of her way so she could stay the near the door. At last a fat man with a cigar stub hanging from his lip opened the door.

"Line up," he growled. The girls pushed forward. The fat man grumbled to himself and frowned around the cigar as he filled each girl's sack with apples and accepted her money. Meg paid out the last of the coins she had saved from her apples the day before.

Not many girls in line behind her got apples before the fat man said, "That's all," and slammed the door. Meg felt a surge of relief as she heard his heavy footsteps fading away. Some days, when she was late, she was one of the ones at the back who didn't get apples, but Meg wouldn't think about that.

She hurried back the way they had come with Mole struggling to hold up one side of the heavy sack.

As the sky brightened, the streets filled up with more and more people. The Five Points district of New York, where Meg lived and worked, was one of the most crowded areas of the city. Immigrants fresh from Europe, poor factory workers struggling to earn a buck, and former slaves displaced by the War between the States competed for living space and jobs. On nearly every corner, crippled soldiers begged for a coin from anyone lucky enough to have work. Homeless children, who had been orphaned by the war or on the voyage across the ocean, darted among wagons, horse-drawn buses, and carriages crowding the streets. No one gave a second glance to Meg and Mole as they pushed and squeezed their way through the throngs. It took half an hour to reach the corner where Meg always stood to sell her apples.

A ragged little girl was there already, selling matches. Meg glared at her. "Shove off," she said. "This is my corner."

The match girl, smaller than Meg, moved off without a word.

"Can't I eat just one of the apples?" Mole asked. "Please, Meg? I'm near to starved. I'll keel over if I don't eat something."

"Well, just one."

Mole grinned. He took the biggest apple he could see and crunched into it sideways, careful of his new loose tooth. Then he sat on the curb, drawing in the muddy gutter with a stick.

"Get up out of that filth," Meg demanded. "You can practice a bit of reading here, before I get too busy."

Mole stood up, but hung back from the post with signs tacked all over it. "It's no use practicing, Meg. I can't read."

"Sure you can read, if you ever once try. Da said anybody could learn it. He taught me."

"I never knew Da. Maybe I'm just too dumb to read."

"Not hardly." Meg sighed. "Ma would be proud of you."

Mole rubbed one bare foot against the other. "But she can't read, and she said it never helped Da much as far as she could see."

Meg shook a finger at him. "Don't be saying things against your Da." She would have said more, but a young boy interrupted her to buy some apples for his mama. When she was done selecting the half dozen apples he wanted, Mole was nowhere to be seen. Meg sighed again. Hadn't she just said as much to Ma? How could she look out for Mole when he never paid her no mind? There was no help for it now, she supposed. He'd come back to find her once he was hungry enough.

Meg called her apples for sale, but it was still early, and not very many people were interested in stopping. She started reading the notices on the gaslight post to pass the time. Most were old notices of men the police wanted, or lyceums coming soon, or shows in Madison Theater. One notice told of a circus over in Brooklyn, set up back in April. She had read all of those so many times she could see them in her sleep. But today a new notice caught her attention. "Orphans," she read, "Find new homes in the West. Plenty of work available--Come to the Children's Aid Society."

"What's that you're so caught up in?"

Meg jumped and turned to face Charlie, the newsboy who sold his papers across from her corner.

"You gave me a start," she grumbled.

Charlie grinned. "What are you reading?"

She read him the notice out loud.

"Children's Aid Society? I've heard of them." He balanced a load of papers on his hip, his grin turned upside down in puzzlement. "They run a couple of lodging houses for the newsboys. What are they doing now?"

Meg shrugged. "Maybe they ran out of room in the lodging houses. I just know they're shipping bummers out West." She shifted her bag of apples to her other shoulder. She had read something about the Children's Aid Society in one of Charlie's papers. A man, Charles Loring Brace, kept saying that the street orphans needed homes with good farm families in the country to grow up right. A lot of people thought he was crazy. Meg was just suspicious. Why would Reverend Brace or anyone else care what happened to the thousands of homeless children in New York? Meg hadn't noticed much sympathy coming her way. "Maybe they want the bummers to starve out there so as to get them off the streets here," she told Charlie. "Clean up some for the quality folk."

"You said good homes. It sounds like a fair deal to me. Maybe I'll go."

Meg snorted. "Good homes? Ha! Who would want the likes of us?"

"Gosh, Meg, you're suspicious of everything. Read today's

headlines for me, won't you, so I can sing it out."

Meg did, as she did every morning. She watched as Charlie crossed the street and began cheerfully calling out, "Fire in Albany; man killed escaping from the burning building. Read all about it!"

She shook her head. That Charlie. He was too happy for his own good.

Mole appeared at her elbow before the day was half over. She gave him a penny to buy a couple of beef dodgers for them both, but he never came back with one for her. By late afternoon, she sold all her apples. She folded up the sack and went hunting for Mole. She found him in an alley, playing at pitching pennies with a group of boys.

"What do you think you're doing?" She dragged him away by an ear, furious at him for gambling. "Where's the penny I gave you for lunch?"

Mole scuffed his bare toes in the dust. "I lost it in the game." He looked up at her through the tangled hair hanging in his face and smiled, a gap tooth grin that usually made her laugh. "But that's all right. Really. I pinched a pork pie at noon."

"You stole it?" Meg whirled on him.

"Sure." Mole hesitated before her unexpected anger. "All the fellas do it."

"Not you!" Meg grabbed him by the shoulders and shook him so fiercely that his teeth rattled. "Don't you ever let me hear of you stealing, not ever! You hear me?" Meg scolded, but she knew Mole was right. Just about everyone she knew stole when they could get away with it. Why not, when some folks had so much, and the rest of them scrabbled to get enough to eat? But unlike Mole, Meg knew it was wrong. Even worse, Meg knew what happened to thieves that got caught. Thieves, even ones as young as Mole, got sent to Blackwell's prison. Meg shuddered, just thinking about that awful place. She shook Mole again to make him listen.

He shrugged away from her. "All right, all right."

Meg turned her back on him and marched off. "Come on now. You've dilly-dallied away the whole morning, and the better part of the afternoon as well. We've got to find you another coat and shoes."

They poked through the trash heaps in back of the tenement houses along Cherry Street and warehouses along the alleys. The first place they tried, a boy a year or so older than Mole chased them away. He was smaller than Meg, but he carried a six inch knife. "Steer clear," he warned, brandishing the knife. "I'm picking rags here."

At the next place a swarm of really little children poked through the trash. Reluctantly they shifted over to make room. Meg didn't find anything, but she wouldn't let herself get discouraged.

Slowly the two of them worked their way on down the alley, grubbing through each bin and pile. At the next to the last bin, they dug out a lump of brown wool. It was a man's coat that hung to Mole's ankles when he put it on. Both sleeves were worn out at the elbow and the buttons were gone.

"Golly, Meg, this is really warm!" Mole spun around, hugging the coat to him.

Meg folded her arms across her chest and eyed him critically. "We'll patch those sleeves, and find a piece of string to tie it shut." Maybe Ma would smile at her, just once, for thinking of Mole.

"Can I keep it then, Meg? Please?"

"Well, it's nothing to crow about, but I guess it'll do." Meg turned from him. Mole was happy, but Ma would never give such a rag a smile. It would be chasing moonbeams to think otherwise. Best not worry about what Ma would say. She never had more than hard words for Meg at any rate.

They searched another hour in the next alley without finding anything worth keeping. One pair of boots were too worn out even for Mole. They had no soles at all. Mole put them on.

"Hey, look at me! I'm the hurdy-gurdy man." He danced around Meg.

She swatted him away. "Quit your fooling," she complained. "There's not much light left."

Gradually the shadows lengthened and the alleys filled with gloomy twilight. Meg decided it was time they headed home. She stopped at a pushcart and bought a loaf of bread and some potatoes.

Mole dragged his feet along behind her.

Jerking his hand to hurry him along, Meg led the way into the alley off Cherry Street. She was tired too and very hungry. From behind them, they heard the rattle of wheels on the cobblestones. There was a squeal of brakes, then a horse's frightened whinny and a high-pitched scream.

Meg's stomach lurched in sudden fear. She dragged Mole back around the corner to the main street. Traffic had stopped. Drivers and cartmen stood on their seats and shouted. In the center of the turmoil, a woman lay face-down, half under the ice wagon. Blood spread in puddle around her head.

The horse reared and squealed in terror at the blood. The driver fought with the horse, swearing at him all the while. A small crowd gathered to stare and whisper. Still dragging Mole, Meg pushed and squirmed to the front of the crowd.

A policeman elbowed his way through. He prodded the woman gently with his nightstick, then rolled her over. Meg gasped and pulled Mole close to her, burying his face in her skirt. But it was too late to keep him from seeing what she already knew.

Ma's eyes were open, staring vacantly. Dead.

Feeling a scream rising within her, Meg turned and ran, never once loosening her grip on Mole.

CHAPTER 3: NOT A SINGLE TEAR

They ran blindly until Meg's side ached and her breath came in ragged gasps. It finally dawned on her that Mole was crying.

"Stop, Meg, please stop," he pleaded.

Meg knew she should listen to him, but she couldn't. She gripped his hand and dragged him along, slowing to a walk, but not stopping.

Finally, Mole collapsed in a heap on the sidewalk. Meg jerked at his hand. He lay limp, too exhausted even to cry. She sat down beside him by the gutter. Her throat hurt. Her stomach churned. But her eyes were dry.

"That was Ma, wasn't it?" Mole spoke in a whisper, not looking up. "She's dead."

Unable to speak, Meg patted his back, as if that would help. They sat close to each other for a long time. Mole lay his head on her lap, and she didn't push him away. The dark grew deeper. The crowds thinned out. Still neither of the children said a word.

She didn't know how long they had been sitting there when Mole brushed his fingers against her shoulder. "I'm hungry, Meg. Let's go home."

Meg shook her head. "What for?" An empty room? But what else could they do? A great weight seemed to be crushing her, making

23

it hard to breath.

But there were no other choices. With a heavy sigh, Meg got up and led the way.

Jake was there, of course. When they came in, he looked up from his beer and studied Mole's tear-streaked face and Meg's blank, wooden look. "So you heard." His hand shook as he lifted the mug. "Not a single tear for your ma, girl? Can't say I'm surprised." He took a swig and wiped his mouth on the back of his mangled hand. Meg could tell he'd been drinking for hours. "This is my place now," he went on. "And I won't take any lip from you two."

Meg's chin jerked up, but she didn't answer him.

"Don't worry." Jake laughed bitterly. "I won't turn you out. So long as you do as I say, we'll get along just fine. I owe her that much at least." His voice trailed off.

Meg scowled. He owed Ma a lot more than that.

Jake was looking at the bag on Meg's arm. "What have you got there?" When she didn't answer, Jake grabbed the bag from her and dumped the contents on the table. "Nothing but bread and potatoes," he grumbled. "Well, it's something, I guess. Step to it, girl, and fix us some supper. It's late."

Was it only yesterday Meg had said she'd die before cooking for Jake? How was she to guess Ma would do the dying? The slam of the door that morning, cutting off the sound of Ma's sobbing, echoed in her head. Meg gripped the back of the chair to steady herself.

Jake gulped another mouthful of beer. "No one claimed the body." He stared at his mangled hand. "I got no money to pay for it, so there won't be any funeral. She never got paid at the factory this week, but they won't let me claim her wages."

"Don't talk about her that way. Just don't talk about her." Meg's hands shook so hard the chair rattled.

Paying no mind to her, Jake put his head in his hands, talking so low Meg could barely hear him. "She'll be buried in a pauper's grave, nameless, with none to witness. She deserves more, but it don't matter to her anymore. A fine woman she was, a fine woman."

Jake lifted his head, and his eyes focused on Meg. "What are you staring at?" He swiped the back of his hand across his face. "A fine woman like her never deserved you brats. Her children never gave her the least bit of kindness. And you not even crying for her." He shook his head and drained his mug.

Meg tried to shut her ears to him. What could she do? She didn't have enough money to claim the body either. Her eyes burned with unspilled tears. Ma would be ashamed of her still. 'I can't, Ma,' she screamed in her mind. 'I want to, but I can't!' When she closed her eyes, she could see Ma's face, glaring at her. 'Always thinking of yourself,' Ma seemed to say.

Meg shuddered. She never had been able to explain to Ma what she felt. Best to forget about Ma now. Forget all the hurt and anger and shame. Better not to think at all. She took a deep, ragged breath and sliced the potatoes to fry. Mole needed to eat.

He huddled on the bed, looking smaller than ever. He sniffled and wiped his nose on his sleeve, leaving a smear across his face.

"Stop that noise, kid." Jake stared into his empty mug.

Mole's breath caught in a shuddering sob.

"I said stop snivelling!" Jake said. "Or I'll give you something to cry about." He stood up, knocking his chair over. "Your Ma always was too soft on you. You ought to learn something from your sister here. You got to be hard to grow up a man." Jake smacked him across the face. Mole squealed and cringed back further.

"Leave him alone," Meg screamed. She jumped at Jake.

He flicked his fist. The back-handed swipe caught her on the chin like a blow from a hammer. She reeled across the room, hit Ma's bed, and crumpled. Jake picked up Mole by the shirt collar and slapped him. "Stop your crying," he demanded again, but Mole was too scared to hear him.

Furious beyond thinking, Meg jumped at Jake again, biting, scratching and kicking. He hit her again, like a cat batting at a fly. She crumpled to the floor, too dizzy to focus.

Jake dropped Mole and came after her. She couldn't move out of his reach. He stood over her, hitting her face open-handed until her cheeks burned. Meg struggled to free herself, to turn aside, but he was too strong. She closed her eyes and drowned in the rain of blows.

Finally, he hauled her to her feet. "Don't ever try to fight me, girl. I make the rules now. Your Ma let the pair of you run wild, and I'm not about to do that."

Meg clenched her teeth to keep from crying out and balled her hands into fists to keep from shaking. She was so angry that she barely noticed the throbbing pain in her jaw.

He held her, shaking his head. "Still not a tear from you, not for your own Ma, not for anything. Hard as iron, you are." He pulled her face right up to his own. "Don't you know iron cracks and breaks?"

Meg stared at him without a word. Imagine the likes of him judging her. He could have done right by Ma. His sadness came too late.

Jake scowled at her, his fist raised to hit her again. Then all the fire went out of his eyes. He lowered his fist and let go of her. "Get my supper," he ordered. He sounded as if he were just as tired as she was. He set the chair up and sat.

Her cheeks still burning, Meg fried the potatoes. She divided them into three equal portions and put one plate in front of Jake.

Jake took Mole's plate from her and dumped half of it onto his own. "He don't need so much," he said. "Seeing as he's about knee high to a skeeter."

"He can have mine." Meg kept her voice steady.

"No, he can go hungry. Time he started helping earn his keep."

Meg clenched and unclenched her fists deep in her skirt pocket. She had said as much earlier, but it was not Jake's place to be saying so. Her throat hurt with holding in the tears.

After eating, Jake lay down and went to sleep right away. Mole curled up on the other bed as far away from Jake as he could get. Meg lay down beside him. She waited until she heard Jake's rattling snores before touching Mole.

"You awake?" she whispered. She felt him nod. "Here." She passed him a piece of bread she had saved in her pocket.

Without a word, Mole shoved it in his mouth. He chewed and swallowed, then curled up almost on top of her. She didn't push him away. Soon he was sleeping too.

Unable to sleep, Meg gripped the thin mattress as if it could hold her in place. The thoughts locked in her head spun round and round until she was dizzy. Ma was dead. Ma couldn't take care of them anymore.

But Ma hadn't taken care of them for years now, not really. So why did she feel so lost? Nothing had really changed, had it?

Meg drew a deep, shuddering breath, but she didn't cry. Ma would call her hard and unfeeling. Was Ma right? Was it all her fault?

She rolled over, kicking the cover off. Her stomach felt wound into a hard knot. She replayed the argument she'd had with Ma. Maybe if she had never talked back to her, maybe if she'd had a kind word or a goodbye for her, maybe Ma would still be alive.

Meg inched away from Mole. Even though the coal fire was out, the air was hot and stuffy. The smell of Jake's beer and sweat filled the room. Rats skittered in the walls. Meg sat up, but there was nowhere to go. She lay back down.

Trapped. Like Ma, she was doomed to live in misery or die from it. Forever making mistakes. She could have called out to Da that night and made him stay home. She could have gone to Ma that morning and said she was sorry. Maybe Ma would have been more careful coming home. Meg groaned. Why did she always say the wrong thing?

She tossed and turned all night and then woke late the next morning. She touched Mole's cheek, waking him. With a finger to her lips, she warned him to be quiet. Jake never stirred as they slipped out the door.

Mole tagged along, dragging his feet. He fussed about being hungry and hung onto her like he thought she might disappear.

What with her oversleeping and his dawdling, she came late to the apple warehouse. The apple man had already shut the door. She went to the match warehouse where she sometimes got matches to sell, but they had already passed out as many as they had for the day. She wandered the alleys searching trash heaps for rags she could sell. She found nothing. Younger children jostled her, but she barely noticed.

What now? The question nagged at her as much as Mole did. She had no answer for either of them.

Noon came. She hadn't earned a penny. Her stomach rumbled angrily. Mole dragged along behind her. When dusk fell they returned to the tenement off Cherry Street, with nothing in the bag.

Jake waited, arms crossed and foot tapping with impatience. "What did you do the day long?" he snarled. "Did you figure to give up working? I told you I wouldn't be letting the pair of you run wild like your Ma did. I aim to do right by her."

"What do you care what Ma would want?" Meg snapped. "She

never wanted you to hit us, but that never stopped you."

Jake's open hand stung against her cheek, but she didn't flinch. Let him do his worst. It didn't matter. Nothing could hurt more than the ache inside of her.

Jake raised his hand again, but stopped. For a moment their eyes locked. Then he dropped his hand and slammed the chair against the table. "I got better things to do then play nursemaid to a couple of brats," he growled. "Just be sure you start bringing home meat if you want a place to stay the night." He stomped out, slamming the door behind him.

CHAPTER 4: WHEN IS IT STEALING?

In the days following their mother's death, Mole clung to Meg all day. He leaned against her leg while she stood selling the apples, and squeezed up against her in the bed each night till she felt suffocated.

"Go on and pick rags," she told him every morning. But he never did.

"Don't be such a crybaby." That only made him cry more. He sniffled all the time and wiped his nose on the sleeve of the new coat, where his arms hung out the holes at the elbows. Meg never had the time or the will to fix them.

The last Saturday in September was a dreary day and the apples didn't sell well. She had just enough money to buy a few potatoes for supper, but nothing more, not even a bit of bread.

Jake pounced on her the minute she came through the door. "You lazy chit!" He fumed, gripping her arm and shaking her. "Did you know rent was due yesterday? Landlord said we gotta pay or get out. Why didn't you tell me?"

Meg shrugged. "I told Ma," she said, too tired to fight him. She gave him half the coins she had saved to buy apples the next day.

Jake snatched the coins from her and scowled. "This ain't half enough." He raised his hand.

Meg stared defiantly at him. What difference did it make if he hit her again?

Jake cursed and lowered his hand. "You don't give a tinker's damn if we get turned out, do you? Not even if I beat you, not even for your own Ma that died. Not for nothing." Jake resumed his pacing. Three steps table to bed, three steps back again. Meg watched silently. He stopped short in front of her and stared at her again. "You're a hard one, girl. But you're no match for me. Give me your boots."

"What?" Meg jerked back and scowled.

"Your boots. I'll pawn them for the rent. They're good boots, and it won't hurt someone tough as you to go barefoot a bit." He snapped his fingers and held out his hand. "Hurry up."

With narrowed eyes and lips pursed in fury, Meg untied her boots. One by one, she pulled them off and handed them to Jake.

Boots in hand, Jake strode out of the room.

"I'm hungry, Meg." Mole piped up after the door closed. He no longer spoke when Jake was in the room.

Meg fried the potatoes on the coal burner and gave most of them to Mole. Her stomach twisted in a knot too tight for swallowing.

They ate all the potatoes without a word. Meg wondered if Jake would be angry they didn't leave any for him, but she couldn't bring herself to care. She wiped the pan clean, while Mole sat on the floor and played with his roach trap.

"Leave that alone. I'm turning out the light now."

"I'm not tired." Mole set his trap under the bed and scooted over close to the wall.

"Well, and it's no wonder you're not tired, with you just sitting the day long, but I am. Now go to sleep." Meg turned down the wick on the oil lamp, plunging the room into darkness. She stepped around the table to join Mole in bed.

"Tell me a story, like Ma used to when I was little. Please, Meg."

Meg remembered. Ma used to tell him stories of the bogeyman and send him squealing to bed. But now the bogeyman was too real, and she didn't want to think of that kind of story. "I'm too tired for stories." The only light in the room came from the faint glow of the dying coal fire. As her eyes adjusted to the dim, she could just make out her brother's face. His eyes were wide open.

He was quiet for a few minutes. Then he touched her hand. "I caught bunches of cockroaches tonight, Meg, bunches. Almost as many as yesterday. I put them in the matchbox under the bed. But he'll just squash them all again, every single one of them, like he did last night." Mole's voice shook.

"Don't be fretting after a bunch of bugs. You ought to just leave them alone anyhow." She wiped his damp cheeks with the blanket edge.

He lay still another minute or two. "Meg?" he whispered. "Are you awake?"

"No. It's time to sleep." She turned her back to him.

He tapped her shoulder. "It's so dark, Meg. Is it this dark in heaven?"

Meg rolled back over and put her arm around him. "You hush now. I'll tell you Da's faery story. It started back when Da was a young man in Ireland."

Meg remembered sitting on Da's lap as he told the story. Back then she still believed there could be magical places, like Ireland. She sighed. Believing in that nonsense wouldn't help Mole now, but she couldn't bear his fretting about dying. She went on with the story.

"Da said 'tis a country filled with little people, the faeries. They always played tricks on people, like riding the pig all night or milking the cow before the farm wife could. Well, these faeries had been plaguing Da's family for a whole winter, turning one thing after another sour. Finally, Da got so mad, he said he would find those faery folk and make them pay. He set a trap in the woods by a faery hill, and he hid behind a big rowan tree."

"What's a rowan tree?" Mole pushed the blanket away and sat up. "Is it like those trees they sell at Christmas time? The ones that prick your fingers if you grab on?"

"It's some kind of special tree what the faeries don't like. But not like those. There aren't any rowan trees here, only in Ireland." Truth was, Meg didn't know exactly what a rowan tree was or why Da thought it was so special, but it's what Da had said. She just told it his way.

"Can it hurt you?"

"Da didn't mind it. I guess people don't have to worry about such trees." Meg patted the mattress.

Instead of lying back down, Mole sat with his back against the wall. He twisted his hands nervously. "Is it magic?"

"Never mind about that tree. Do you want me to tell the story or not?"

"I want you to tell it."

"All right, then." Meg closed her eyes a minute to think where she had stopped, then went on. "When the moon came up big and round, Da saw the faeries come out of a hidden door. They danced around the ring, just as he knew they would. One of them spied the trap and went over to it. The faery touched it, and it caught him fast.

"In a twinkling, Da stood up and said, 'I've caught you now, and you'll be paying the forfeit.' All the other faeries disappeared in a flash.

"The one in the trap shrieked and cursed at Da. 'You'll never be leaving faery land now,' the faery warned. 'You'll be enchanted for sure.'

"But Da had thought ahead. He pointed to the rowan tree. 'You can't work your magic on me so long as I'm touching this, as well you know.'

"And indeed the faery did know, so he tried to win Da over with sweetness and cunning. 'Please, kind sir, just let me go free, and I'll be leading you to a treasure the like of which you've never even dreamed of.'

"Da knew better than to trust that promise! 'First the treasure, then I'll set you free,' he demanded.

"That old faery fussed and fumed and pleaded and promised. But Da knew all his tricks, and at last the faery knew he was beaten. With a snap of his magic fingers, that faery dug up his pot of gold and gave it to Da, and Da set him free.

"Now Da knew that faery would be after his gold again, so he gathered up Ma, who was waiting to marry him, and with the gold they came to America. And they always had good luck here." Meg finished the story with Da's words, but the story had gone sour. What kind of luck had any of them had since Da died?

Mole leaned forward, his eyes glistening in the shadowy room. "What happened to the pot of gold?"

"Nothing." She pushed him down and tucked the blanket under his chin. "There's no pot of gold. There never was. It's just a faery story. There's no faeries in America." She turned her back to him once more. "Go to sleep."

In the third week after Ma died, Meg and Mole returned to the tenement room to find the door locked against them. It had rained that day, and both of them were dripping. A puddle spread at their feet as Meg pounded on the door. She could hear Jake's voice inside, along with another voice, a woman's voice. Meg pounded again.

"Go away," Jake growled through the closed door. "You got no place here anymore. No one can expect me to play daddy to a couple of ungrateful brats."

Mole pulled on her sleeve. "I'm hungry."

"Hush your whining. Can't you never think of anything besides your belly?" She should have expected this, she guessed. Jake had been grumbling about it since Ma died, since he'd paid the rent with the money from her boots. But where could they go now? She sat down with her back against the door and tucked her bare feet up inside her dress.

Mole sat beside her. "What are we going to do, Meg?"

"Just hush," she snapped. "Why are you always asking me that? You're more trouble then you're worth."

Mole's eyes widened in fear. "Are you going off and leaving me too, Meg?"

"Who said anything about leaving you? Just hush and let me think." She ran her fingers through his snarled hair. What did she care about a dirty and airless room? They had nothing to hold them there.

Then she remembered Ma's basket under the bed. Not much there; just a few pins and needles, a spool of thread and the Bible that had belonged to Da. Ma never looked at it, but Meg had. All that was hers by rights. She stood up and kicked the door.

"Go away," Jake snarled. "I told you. You got no place here anymore."

"We'll be going," Meg called through the door. "Just as soon as we collect Ma's things. You got no right to them."

"Just give the beggars the things, Jake," the woman said.

Meg heard the bed creak and Jake's heavy footsteps crossing the floor. She heard him fumble with the key in the lock, then the door flew open.

"Hurry up then," he said.

Meg ducked under his arm to slip inside the familiar apartment. Already it smelled different, with a delicate perfume Ma had never known. The woman sat on Ma's bed, with the thin blanket wrapped around her.

Meg crawled under the bed and dragged out Ma's wicker sewing basket. An empty whiskey bottle lay on top of it. Meg felt a chill pass through her, seeing the ghost of Ma lingering on the bed, the empty whiskey bottle in her hand. Meg looked away, before she heard again the angry words that last morning.

That's when she saw it. On the table, next to the oil lamp, was a gold pocket watch. She glanced at Jake but he had forgotten her already, his arms wrapped around the woman on the bed. The watch glinted in the smoky light, just inches from her hand. Meg closed her fist around the watch and slipped it into the sewing basket. Then, with her heart beating wildly, she walked out the door.

As soon as the door closed, she grabbed Mole's hand and ran down the dark hallway. Nearby a baby cried, and a couple argued in loud, strident voices. A drunk sang in an off-key Irish brogue. No one heard the two children stumbling their way through the foul-smelling halls, down the rickety steps and outside into the clear night air.

"Where are we going, Meg?" Mole struggled to keep up with her. The moon, a dull orange, hung low in the sky overhead. A breeze lifted a crumpled newspaper and blew it across the empty alley.

She didn't answer. "Don't steal," she had warned Mole. Kellys don't steal.

But it wasn't really stealing, was it? Jake owed it to her. He could have sold that instead of her boots. It should be hers, by rights, since her boots had gone for the rent, and the room was no longer theirs. Like Da and his pot of gold. He had taken that from the faery. Why shouldn't she take the watch from Jake?

"Where are we going, Meg?" Mole asked again as they left Cherry Street behind. An empty street car at the end of its run rattled past.

"We got to find a new place to sleep the night. And don't you worry about leaving that old room behind, since we're no more than saying goodbye to bad rubbish." Meg tried to reassure herself as well

34

as her brother. If she could just take care of him, she'd be all right. That was what Ma always said, wasn't it? Meg held tight to Mole's hand. "We'll count ourselves lucky to be away from that man." She wouldn't think about the watch now. No sense fretting over it. For good or bad, it was done.

"But where, Meg?" Mole insisted.

"Just hush, and let me figure it out." She hadn't thought about this. She hadn't had time to make any plans. "I guess for tonight we'll sleep out. It's not too cold. We'll just find someplace dry. We can look for new digs tomorrow." She looked over her shoulder. No one had followed them, but she held tightly to Mole's hand and walked a little faster.

When would Jake notice the watch was gone? Would he guess she had taken it?

They walked four or five blocks in silence. The street, never empty, was a bit quieter now, with most people at home enjoying their suppers. Meg knew a lot of bummers with nowhere to sleep, Charlie for one. He usually paid a penny for a bed at one of the boy's lodging houses run up by churches or groups like the Children's Aid Society. Meg had heard some bummers talk about sleeping on the grates, where the heat came up from the buildings. She and Mole might try that.

They couldn't find an empty place. They walked for ten blocks up and down Cherry Street and every alley and side street in the Five Points District. Ragged children huddled together in clumps of three or four on every grate. There was no room for Meg and Mole. Meg's legs ached. Mole walked slower with each step.

"Can't you just walk?" Meg jerked him along.

"I'm tired," Mole whined.

"And you're thinking I'm not?" Meg asked. He would fall asleep on his feet soon, and she'd have to carry him. She wasn't sure she could manage that. Meg wanted nothing more than to collapse where they were. But she couldn't do that, and she wouldn't leave him behind. "Not much further," she coaxed. "We'll find someplace soon."

But they walked for another hour before Meg found a rickety staircase fire escape at the end of a narrow alley. The staircase had been partially blocked off and hidden by old boxes. It seemed no one else had found it yet.

Meg pulled Mole underneath. The wooden steps had kept most of the day's rain off the ground below, and the dirt was nearly dry. Without a word, the children curled up close to each other for warmth and finally slept.

CHAPTER 5: JUST ANOTHER DREAM

Morning dawned cold and overcast, a gray day threatening more rain. Meg stood up and stamped her cold feet to get the blood moving. She shook Mole awake and took him onto her lap. "I'm a fool." Her hands shook as she tore strips of cloth off her apron and wrapped them around his feet. "I should have done this last night."

"I'm hungry," Mole whined as she wound the cloth around her own feet the same way.

"Isn't that a wonder?" Meg said sourly. No supper last night, and not likely to find much for breakfast this morning. She shook her head. "We'll have apples soon."

Mole sat with his back against the brick wall under the staircase, his skinny arms wrapped around his knees, pulling them up to his chest under his tattered overcoat. "I can't be walking with nary a bite to eat, Meg."

"Do you see any food here?" Meg waved her arm in a wide, sweeping gesture that took in the whole alley, piled high with old boxes.

Mole shook his head slowly, but made no move to get up.

Meg yanked him to his feet. "Then you'll have to be walking with nary a bite to eat, so we can get some food." She didn't let go of his hand all the way to the apple warehouse.

As soon as Meg got her apples, she gave one to Mole. He ate the whole thing, core and all, before they got to her corner.

"Can I have another apple?" Mole reached toward the open bag.

Meg held it up high. "Da used to say a fellow ought to whistle for his supper."

Mole puckered up his lips and blew. A breathy squeak came out through the gap of his missing tooth.

"You call that a whistle?" Meg teased. "It sounds more like a dying rat. Put your tongue against your teeth, like this." She whistled one clear note.

Mole squeezed his eyes tight shut and blew as hard as he could. This time the squeak sounded like the wind swirling through their alley. It ended with his lips flapping.

Meg laughed.

Mole slapped his fist against his thigh and frowned. "I don't guess I'll ever whistle." He plunked himself down on the curb.

Meg sat beside him. "Maybe you can't whistle yet." She poked him in the ribs, tickling first one side, then the other. "But I bet you can giggle." She tickled him again.

Mole squirmed as he struggled to get away from her. "Leave me go," he gasped, breaking into giggles.

A young woman in a crisp white pinafore cleared her throat. "Seems to me you would sell more apples if you paid attention to your customers. How much are you charging?"

Meg let go of Mole to help the housemaid select the apples she needed for her family. When she finished, Mole was drawing pictures in the mud by the gutter.

"Can't I please have another apple, Meg?" Mole clutched his stomach. "My belly's shrunk up all the way to my back."

"Forget about your stomach just a bit, Moley. Here try reading this notice." She pointed to the sign post on the corner. "It's about a circus."

"I don't want to read about any circus I can't even see. I'm awful hungry, Meg. Just one more apple?"

"If I give you the apples, I can't sell them." Her voice was sharp with frustration. "Stop your begging. If you're so hungry, go pick rags and earn a little something to help us out."

Mole took a few steps away from Meg, then darted back to her. "We're not going back to Jake are we?"

"Not hardly." Meg felt the weight of the watch in her apron pocket. More likely he'd come after them.

Mole smiled. "That's okay then." He skipped off. Meg watched as Mole slipped nimbly through the crowds filling the streets. She doubted he would pick rags. But for the first time in weeks, he wasn't clinging to her.

She spent all day selling her apples. As the sky darkened and the first few gaslights winked on, Mole still hadn't come back. Worried, Meg went looking for him. She tried the trash heaps along several of the alleys and even looked down at the River. Then she wandered up past the Girls' Lodging House near Five Points Mission. The place was run by the Children's Aid Society, the same outfit sending orphans out west. On the door, they had another notice about homes for orphans. Next to that was a broadsheet telling about night school. Free and open to working girls, the advertisement claimed.

Meg laughed bitterly. Free? What about books and pencils and clothes to wear? No, school was nothing but another useless dream, not for the likes of her.

She found Mole in the alley off Cherry Street, playing stick ball. "Mole!" she called sharply. When he didn't come, she pushed in among the boys, grabbed his collar, and dragged him away. "I thought I told you to do something useful." How could he be so foolish, playing here in their old alley? What if Jake saw him? Anger and fear boiled inside of her. She shook him hard.

"I tried, Meg, but no one threw away anything good today." He smiled his gap-toothed grin. "But a lady gave me a penny, and I bought some corn at noon."

Meg shook him again. "So now you're begging too." She turned her back on him and stalked out of the alley.

Mole caught up to her and pulled on her skirt. "I'm hungry." He stuck his hand in hers. "That corn was hours ago."

Meg sighed and ruffled his hair. "So what else is new?" She teased. "Come along. There are still peddlers out on Broadway."

Meg bought a hot pasty for each of them. Then she counted their money. "There's not enough for a room." She closed her hand around the solid weight of the watch hidden in her pocket. She could sell it now and buy a room for the night. Even at the pawn shop the watch would give them enough to buy a bed for weeks. "And then what?" the nagging voice in her head said. No, best hang onto the watch until they really needed it. "We'll have to bum again tonight," she told Mole.

"It's okay." Mole shrugged. "At least it doesn't smell as bad out here." He wrinkled up his nose, like a rat.

Meg laughed and swatted at him, pushing him off balance. "Go on. We ought to be calling you 'Ratty' instead of Mole."

The sky cleared as it grew darker. A few stars blinked over the city that was never quite dark, never quite asleep. Pools of light spilled out through loosely shuttered windows on the main street and spread to the edges of the alleys. Under the staircase it was darker, but the footsteps of constables and raucous laughter coming in bursts from the taverns kept Meg awake long after Mole had curled up with his head on her lap.

The weather continued fine for all that first week. Meg soon gave up looking for someplace else. There was never quite enough at the end of the day to do much more than feed them. She saved a bit each night, but the pennies didn't count up very fast. Each night after Mole was asleep, she took out the watch and wound it. It was their pot of gold, she told herself. It would bring them luck. But she didn't let Mole see it, and she never held it long. As she stared at it, a knot of fear grew in her belly like a stone. Would Jake be looking for her?

During the day, Mole ranged from the wharves on the East River to Broadway and Five Points, playing stick ball and crack the whip with a gang of boys Meg didn't know. She saw them daring each other to hop on the horse cars, and Meg knew they pitched pennies in the alleys whenever they could find a coin or two. Meg gave him a penny once for him to buy lunch for the two of them, but he came back with neither penny nor food, so she didn't do that again. Usually Mole came to meet her before she finished selling apples, but when he didn't she gave up looking for him. They would meet under the staircase to eat a potato or a bit of bread before sleeping.

One day, Mole came to the staircase with three other boys. Two were Mole's size, but the third was older, almost as tall as Meg.

"This is our place," Meg said warily.

"It's okay, Meg. This is Dicer." Mole pointed to the biggest boy first. "And Billy and Sam. They're my friends."

"I told you not to tell anybody anything about where we slept." Meg narrowed her eyes at the intruders.

"There's plenty of room." Sam shrugged and pulled his cap down over his ears. "It's no skin off your nose."

Meg glared at them all, including Mole. She might be able to drive off one or two, but not all three, and not without Mole's help. "Just don't be expecting me to feed the lot of you," she said at last.

As the night turned even colder, Meg wasn't sorry for the extra bodies, but she didn't trust Dicer, with his dark eyes flicking back and forth, missing nothing. She didn't take the watch out that night, not even to wind it.

The next night, Mole came back early and alone. One eye was black and puffy.

"What happened?" Meg demanded.

Mole crawled onto her lap. "Dicer said you would leave me someday, and I lit into him. But he's way bigger than me." Mole rubbed his eyes with his fists, smearing the tears and dirt together. "You won't leave me, Meg, will you? I told him you wouldn't do that, and he laughed."

"No, I won't leave you. We'll stick together like fleas on a dog." She hugged him close to her as if to demonstrate. "But don't you go fighting bigger boys anymore. You'll get yourself killed. Then how could I stick with you? You'd put me in a pretty mess!"

Mole laughed a little and wiped his nose on his jacket. He held on to her.

"Here, now." Meg pushed him away. "I saved you some bread."
Mole stuffed it in his mouth.

"Oh, Moley, whatever am I gonna do with you?" Meg worried.

Mole just smiled. "I found another beetle today. A shiny black
one. Want to see it?"

The next day a soft drizzle dripped from the leaden sky for
hours. Meg stood on her corner shivering, but by nightfall, she still had
half of her apples left. Cold and wet, she went back to their staircase
without bread or anything hot to eat.

Mole was already there. Tears rolled down his grimy cheeks and
dripped onto his soggy jacket.

"What is it now?" Meg asked wearily.

"I was so hungry. Dicer and me, we decided to pinch some hot
corn. Only a copper saw us." Mole sniffed, then wiped his nose with
the back of his hand. "He chased me. I ran and ran, until I couldn't run
no more. I thought sure he was gonna get me. Oh, Meg, I promise I
won't never steal no more!"

"And haven't I heard that promise before?" Meg said. "Sure
you'll be in Blackwell's prison before you're half grown."

Mole slumped on the ground and pulled his knees up to his
chest under the coat. "I mean it this time, Meg. Honest!"

Meg pulled him onto her lap. Sitting on the cold, wet ground,
she rocked him back and forth, like she had when he was a baby. Drops
of rain slid through the wooden slat steps of the staircase and plopped
on their bent heads and the ground around them. Mole's small body
leaning against her seemed to be the only spot of warmth in the whole
world. "You ought to stay away from that Dicer," she said at last. "He's
nothing but trouble."

"Would they really send me to Blackwell's Island, Meg, if they
caught me? That's where Dicer's big brother is."

Meg shook her head. "Maybe not. Maybe you're too little yet,
and they would only send you to the Orphan's Asylum. Not that that's
a fair sight better."

Both children knew the big prison-like building which served
as an orphanage for the city. It was a grim, forbidding place and the

42

orphans who lived there looked thin and gray.

"You just be careful. Don't be pinching anything. You hear me?" Meg thought of the watch in her pocket. That's different, she told herself. Jake owed it to us. But she didn't show it to Mole.

Mole was sound asleep by the time Dicer, Charlie, and Sam joined them an hour later. Meg didn't say a word against them. They were warmer with the five of them together.

That night, the drizzle turned to sleet, and then a soft, wet snow. Meg couldn't keep from shivering. Her belly ached with worry. It was only October, far too early for snow. How would they ever get through the winter?

Mole's breathing was ragged, and he coughed in great spasms, waking himself up and moaning.

Meg finally sat up, with Mole's head in her lap. It couldn't go on like this. She had already sold Ma's Bible, the sewing needles, and even the basket to buy food. Was it time to sell the watch? She pulled it out of her pocket and stared at the beautiful, shiny gold. But Meg had sold enough rags and bits of junk in her life to know that even a gold watch wouldn't buy them warm clothes and food and a place to sleep all winter. Then, with their treasure gone, what would they do? Sink into bitterness like Ma had done?

Her leg had gone to sleep. Shifting Mole over a bit, Meg rubbed her sore feet, numb with cold. Maybe she could get a job, a good job, like a housemaid, up on Fifth Avenue. Nancy, who used to sell hot roasted corn a couple of blocks away from Meg, had managed to find a place with policeman's family. Surely, scrubbing and sweeping couldn't be all that hard. A job like that would pay plenty for hot food every day and decent digs.

Early the next morning, the snow was still falling. The sky loomed a dull gray promising more snow. Meg untangled herself from the jumble of arms and legs. She stood up and stamped her feet and waved her arms to warm up.

The snow stuck in patches on the steps and trash barrels, but mostly it had melted into a black, muddy slush. Meg sat on the bottom step of the staircase, which served as their roof, and rewrapped the rags covering her feet. She knew they would be soaked through in no time, but rags were still better than nothing.

Maybe she could use the watch to buy boots. Would it bring enough for boots for Mole too? Meg didn't know. Selling it seemed like a big risk. Better to think of a job first.

"Morning, Meg." Mole shivered and rubbed his arms briskly, then coughed. He pulled his jacket tighter. "Geez, it's snowing! Want to have a snowball fight? After breakfast, I mean. I'm starved."

Dicer sat up and grinned. "Ain't we all?" He shook his friends awake. "C'mon. Let's get something to eat." He led the way out of the alley.

"Wait, Mole," Meg called him back as he started to follow the other boys. "You stay with me today."

"Meg! Do I have to?"

"Where are they going to get breakfast?" Meg set her hands on her hips. "You tell me that. Are they going to buy it?"

Mole scowled down at his toes.

"I thought you said you weren't never gonna steal no more." Meg hammered away at him, even though she could tell he had shut his ears. "You want to end up in Blackwell's?"

"Aw, Meg, I don't want to be a chicken neither. Everybody pinches food. I didn't get caught."

Meg grabbed his shoulders and shook him. "Not us. Not the Kellys. You be careful of that Dicer. He's no good. You think he'd come back and help you, if you got caught?"

"He's my friend, Meg."

"He's no kind of friend as I can see." Gripping his wrist, she led him out of the alley. "I'll get us some bread. And I won't have to steal it." She ignored the weight of the watch in her pocket.

Mole looked longingly after his friends, but Meg jerked him after her. She led him all the way uptown, past the slums and broken down tenements toward fashionable Fifth Avenue. The drizzle started up again, a light sprinkling of rain mixed with sleet, just enough to keep them damp and cold.

The streets were less crowded as they headed uptown. There were no beggars on the corners and fewer peddlers. Meg walked past rows of elegant brownstone homes. She watched the businessmen in dapper new suits and hats emerge and stride confidently off to work. Meg had never been inside a house like these. She wondered what it was like. Clean, she imagined, and bright. The lacy curtains she saw at every window wouldn't keep out the light.

"What are we doing?" Mole asked, after they had walked past the same row of houses three times. "You said we could eat."

"Hush up." Meg stopped to watch a carriage pull up.

A footman stood holding the door. He scowled at her. "Be off with you," he warned. "We want no beggars around here."

Meg jerked her chin up like she had been hit and glared at him. "I'm not doing you any harm."

The footman raised his fist. "You've no business loitering here. Be off with you, or I'll call the police."

She grabbed Mole's hand, spun on her heel, and led him briskly away. At the end of the row, Meg stopped to look back.

A lady with her two small sons came out of the house. The little boys, dressed in spotless white shirts, and matching blue jackets and trousers, skipped ahead of their mama into the carriage. The lady followed more slowly. She stepped in, careful to keep her soft, peach-colored dress out of the mud. She smoothed down her skirts over her petticoats and arranged herself neatly before motioning the footman to close the door.

Meg turned away, jerking Mole after her. She could never get a job at one of these places. They would laugh if they didn't throw her out before she even asked. 'What, a filthy slum girl in a big house?' No. They would have to count the china and the silver every day, and they would claim she brought in more dirt than she cleaned. Meg jerked at Mole's hand again, hurrying him away, back to the Five Points district.

"What was that all about?" Mole complained. "I'm tired."

"Nothing," Meg answered without looking at him. "Nothing but a worthless dream." She was furious with herself. She ought to know about dreams by now. Ma had known. Dreaming wasn't worth anything.

It was too late to get apples, but Meg had some left from the day before. Out of habit, Meg went toward her regular corner. She could get some corn for them nearby. Mole dawdled behind her. Meg waited for him impatiently, glancing ahead to look for any vendors poaching on her territory.

There, on her corner, stood Jake, talking with the newsboy.

Meg spun Mole around, and they ran. Mole was too startled to even cry out.

To Meg's intense relief, Jake hadn't seen them. Meg made Mole run a couple of blocks, then let him slow down.

"Geez, Meg, what did you do that for?" Mole panted.

"Never you mind. Look, there's a corn cart ahead." She bought two ears of corn and gave them both to Mole.

"Ain't you hungry?" he asked between bites.

Meg shook her head. She was too upset to eat.

"Can't I go find Dicer now?" Mole wheedled. "I been following you around all day, and you're just plum crazy."

Meg frowned at him. "You're getting too big to be off playing, and I told you to keep clear of that Dicer."

"I'll be good." Mole backed away from her. "I'll meet you back at the staircase, come dark."

"Mole, wait." Meg grabbed for him, but he turned and scuttled off through the crowd before she could reach him. "Mole, you come back here!" she called, but he paid no attention.

Meg spent the afternoon picking rags, without any luck. As he promised Mole turned up in the alley not long after dark. Dicer and the others followed him and crowded together under the staircase without a word to Meg.

"This is our digs," she said, but she felt too tired to push them out. And she couldn't deny it was warmer with the pack of boys all together.

Still, she couldn't trust Dicer, and Mole's coughing woke her more than once. She dreamt of Jake, his mangled hand clutching her hair as he snarled at her. His mouth gaped open, his blackened teeth gleaming in a skeletal grin. She jerked awake in a cold sweat and found it hard to sleep again.

Finally morning came, as gray and cold as the day before. Meg hesitated before setting off to buy her apples. Was Jake after them? She couldn't be sure. But in the end, it didn't matter if he was or wasn't. She had to work, or they would starve.

"You take care of yourself today, you hear me?" she warned

Mole, before he took off with Dicer and the others. "You steer clear of our old alley."

He grinned. "Don't worry," he boasted. "I'm quicker than a greased cat." He doubled over suddenly in a fit of coughing.

Meg pounded him on the back until the fit passed.

He grinned his gap-toothed grin at her again and ran off.

She scowled after him. She hadn't wanted him clinging all the time, but didn't much like this wild boy he was becoming either. She set about selling her apples, but couldn't help looking over her shoulder all day.

Business was brisk, and by late afternoon she had sold all her apples with no sign of trouble. She stuffed her sack in her apron pocket and turned around.

Too late, she saw Jake.

Before she had time to move, his good hand grabbed her wrist in an tight grip. She screamed, but he clamped his mangled hand over her mouth and muffled it. She kicked and struggled, but couldn't get free. No one passing by paid any attention to the struggling pair.

"You think you can steal from me?" He shook her, snapping her head back. "Give it over."

Suddenly four boys hurled themselves on Jake, kicking, biting, scratching and shrieking, making as much commotion as if there were a dozen of them.

Startled, Jake released his grip just long enough for Meg to slip away. She grabbed for Mole, who was with the boys, and they ran.

The rest of the boys held Jake a moment more, then fled. Jake cursed and kicked at them, before chasing after Meg and Mole.

Meg and Mole ran harder than they had ever run before, up and down twisting alleys. The other boys melted away into side alleys, but Jake kept on after them. Meg knew she could outrun him, but Mole's legs were shorter, and he couldn't stop coughing. In spite of their head start, Jake was gaining on them.

Without slowing, Meg scanned the street ahead of her. Where could she hide? She turned a corner and saw the Girls' Lodging House, run by the Children's Aid Society. She ducked inside. Mole slumped to the floor, hacking and wheezing like an old man.

Meg peered out through the window. Had Jake seen where they

were? With any luck he'd go right on by.

An office door opened. A tall woman dressed in black came out. Mole was still coughing. Meg turned from the window to pound him on the back.

"Can I help you?" the woman asked.

"We want to go west," Meg blurted, remembering the notice she had read there weeks before. She could see Jake on the far corner, looking up and down both streets.

The tall woman smiled. "Come into my office. We'll talk."

Meg took a deep breath, and then another, trying to stop her heart from pounding. She dragged Mole into the office.

CHAPTER 6: NO SUCH THING AS LUCK

"Why do you want to go west?" The tall woman settled herself behind a large desk covered with several stacks of papers.

Meg hesitated. Until that minute, she hadn't wanted to. The whole scheme was nothing but another dream, and she had laughed at Charlie, thinking him a fool to go after it. But she could hardly tell the woman she stole a watch and had to get away. "I heard people out there want orphans. I heard there was work."

The woman nodded. "Yes. There are many families who would love to care for children, in return for your work. Are you orphans? You have no guardians or other family?"

"There's only us." Meg rested her hand on Mole's shoulder. He leaned against her, staring from one face to the other.

"I think we can help you." The woman searched through a stack of papers on her desk until she found the one she wanted. "You'll have to accept the Children's Aid Society as guardians. We'll provide you with coats and shoes." She hesitated. "And, I think, baths."

Meg lowered her eyes and thrust her hands deep in her pockets. She didn't want to be so dirty, but how was she supposed to keep clean living on the streets as she did?

The woman tapped her pencil as she studied the papers in front of her. "We'll arrange transportation to various communities that have indicated they have families who would take in children. You will be able to accept or refuse any family that bids for you, and they will have to agree to see you receive schooling. Our agents will check in with you periodically to see that the family is meeting all obligations and still wants you. Is that satisfactory?"

Meg didn't want to answer. Her head spun with information and questions. Was there really someone who might want her to be part of a family? No one could believe that. But the woman needed an answer now, and somewhere on the other side of the door, Jake was looking for her. She nodded.

"Very well. My schedule says there is a group leaving on Friday, in two days. You can stay here until then."

"What about my brother here?"

"I'm sorry. He'll have to stay at the Orphan's Asylum."

Meg nodded her head again.

"No, Meg, please?" Mole started crying and grabbed her hand. "I want to stay with you. You promised you wouldn't leave me."

Meg spun him around to face her. "Stop your blathering. You're not such a big baby you can't spend two days in the Orphan's Asylum. Would you rather be freezing out in the rain? You've got no more sense than the stupid beetles you catch." She punctuated each word with a quick shake, but she could tell he wasn't listening to her. "Just hush up," she insisted.

The woman came out from behind her desk and put a hand on Mole's shoulder. "Don't worry about your sister. You'll see her again tomorrow and be none the worse for a good night's sleep." She took his hand, but he clung to Meg, his tears falling unchecked.

Meg shook free of him and turned her back as the woman dragged him out of the room. Mole had no business hanging on her like that.

"Sure you're a selfish one." Meg heard the echoes of Ma's words. "Have you no thought for your brother?" Meg stared out the window overlooking the empty street. The gas light at the corner had been lit. Its shadow flickered over the cobbles. Jake was gone, unless he was hiding. Meg shuddered again. She'd not do Mole much good if she were clapped in prison.

In the lodging house, two dozen girls of all ages slept in a large dormitory style room, with bunks lined up along the wall. In spite of the warm bed, Meg didn't sleep well. Dreams of Jake coming after her mingled with dreams of arguing with Ma, and through it all, worry for Mole. Even though she knew he was too far away, with too many walls and streets between them, every time she closed her eyes, she could hear him crying.

She went to see Mole first thing the next morning. His eyes were red rimmed with dark circles underneath. He hurled himself at her the minute he saw her, burying his head in her apron and wrapping his arms around her so tightly she could hardly breathe.

She ruffled his hair. "Hush, now. Didn't I say I'd see you today? It doesn't look like you've come to any harm."

For an answer, Mole just held her tighter.

Mole was not allowed to the leave the Asylum until the day of the trip, but Meg was free to come and go. After a few minutes, she pulled away from Mole's grip on her knees.

"You know I got to go out and work today," she said. "So stop your blathering."

"It's too late to get apples, Meg. Don't go off and leave me." He clutched at her skirt.

One by one, Meg pried his fingers loose. "You know I've got to work. Now leave me alone. I'm coming back." Her stomach clenched uneasily as she spoke. Da had promised to come back too.

She shook her head to clear away the thoughts of Da. She wasn't going off to some fight.

"Meg!" He tried to lock his arms around her legs, clinging like a leech.

She pushed him off and held him at arm's length, so she could squeeze through the door and slam it behind her. She could hear him bawling and kicking the door as she walked down the steps. Meg kicked the railing. Why did he have to make it so hard for her? Wasn't she just telling him yesterday not to take off from her?

Hunching up against the cold wind, Meg picked her way across the icy mud. She walked slowly down the back alleys. Mole was right about one thing. It was too late to sell apples. Little girls were already out skipping rope if they had one, or playing hopscotch in the dirt, but Meg had not done those for years, not since Mole was born and she had been left home to mind him.

She kicked a trash heap beside a tavern door, then wrinkled her nose at the sharp tang of sour beer. She rubbed her sleeve across her face, as if she could wipe away the smell, then bent down to paw through the broken bottles and greasy rags. She might as well look for boots.

Meg worked her way to the bottom of that pile and moved on down the alley to the next heap. A drunk was still sleeping beside a charred barrel. Thin wisps of smoke rose from the trash fire he must have lit the night before.

No point grubbing through that mess. Nothing worth wearing would be left there. At the next heap, a swarm of children pawed their way through the old boards, rotting vegetables, and smashed tins. Meg shrugged and walked on past. She didn't want any trouble.

The morning dragged on. She found nothing but a battered, brown cap that she kept for Mole. By noon, Meg had worked her way down to the wharves by the East River. She sat down on a piling out of the way of the dock workers to watch as they loaded and unloaded the big clipper ships.

Only last summer she and Mole had come here to dunk each other in the water on hot afternoons. At the far end of the dock, Meg saw a ship unloading emigrants from Europe. A clump of them moved toward her. There was a woman carrying a baby wrapped in a filthy blanket. A pack of pasty-faced children clung to her skirt. A man walked beside her, carrying a couple of heavy bags tied together with twine. His eyes darted here and there even more anxiously than the children's.

Meg wondered if that was what Ma and Da had looked liked when they had arrived, fifteen years before. She imagined her father, tall and strong, with his arm around Ma beside him.

It was harder to imagine Ma, young and without the lines of care on her face. Had she been afraid then? Angry and bitter, alone in a new country, with only Da to protect her? Meg couldn't believe Ma had wanted to come.

Meg shook her head. At least Da would be happy for them. "Move on," he would say. "Don't hold back." Da had left Ireland with his pot of gold for luck and never a backward glance.

Meg looked around at the muddy alleys, the dirty wharves and the coarse sailors. Whatever Da said about a pot of gold, it hadn't done him much good, nor Ma either. Meg shivered and wrapped her hand around the gold watch in her pocket. What would it bring her?

She turned away from the emigrants. While she had been sitting there, a chill had settled in her bones, and shadows were growing into each other. She'd dawdled too long.

Before returning to the lodging house, Meg stopped to see Mole and gave him the cap.

He was delighted. "Now I look just like the newsboys. Dicer is going to be a newsboy."

"He's big enough to work now," Meg pointed out. Mole was so taken with his cap, he didn't notice as she slipped off, leaving him there a second night.

Meg slept fitfully again. She woke early and stood outside the office long before the woman arrived to unlock the door.

A tall, gangly girl, a year or two older than Meg joined her, leaning comfortably against the wall as she waited. "If you're heading west, we'll be traveling a long ways together. We might as well start out friendly." She stuck out her hand. "I'm Dorothea McDuff, but most folks call me Dotty."

Dotty's dress, once red, was faded and patched, but her blond hair hung in two neat braids. Her eyes twinkled merrily as if she had just heard a good joke.

Meg shook her hand briefly, but didn't return Dotty's smile. "Meg Kelly," she mumbled.

Meg was spared further conversation by the arrival of the tall woman who had helped them two days earlier. "You're early," she chirped as she unlocked the door. "But I did say early, didn't I? You'll just have to wait a bit while we organize ourselves." She showed them benches in the dark hallway.

Meg sat with Dotty opposite. They waited for a very long time. She closed her eyes and pretended to doze so Dotty wouldn't talk to her.

The secretary brought three girls into the hallway and made introductions. "Take some time to get acquainted. You'll all be traveling together." She went back into her office.

Dotty knelt beside the littlest girl, Nan. She looked to be about four years old. She sniffled and rubbed her fist against her tear-streaked cheeks.

A whiner, Meg thought.

Dotty whispered something in the little girl's ear. Nan smiled a watery smile and climbed onto Dotty's lap.

Josephine, the oldest of the three, sat beside Dotty on the bench and quietly folded her hands in her lap. Her eyes, a dull brown, stared straight and unblinking at the floor in front of her. Mousy hair hung loose and straggly around a pinched face. Meg dismissed her. She was too scared to cause any trouble.

The middle girl, Birdie, caught Meg's attention. She was seven, maybe eight years old, a bit older than Mole. She perched on the edge of the bench for a minute, until the secretary's door closed, then she jumped up and paced up and down the hallway. Her skinny arms and legs seemed too long for her, as if they would fly off on their own if she didn't keep moving. Her eyes flashed angrily at Dotty and Nan, and she kicked at Josephine's boots.

Josephine moved her feet back.

Meg jerked up her chin. She'd do a lot more than move over if that chit tried kicking her.

Finally, the secretary came back, leading a short, very proper lady dressed in a black traveling suit. "This is Miss Firth. She will be accompanying you west. She will see to your needs on the journey and make sure each of you finds a place."

Hands on skinny hips, Birdie planted herself in front of Miss Firth."What for did you keep us waiting here so long?" She let out a string of curses as bad an anything Meg had heard around the worst of the taverns in the Five Points.

If Miss Firth was shocked, she gave no sign of it, nor did she answer. She nodded curtly to the secretary. "Come along, children."

She led them to the wash basin out back and inspected their nails for dirt. She had small brush to help them scrub until Meg's hands tingled. Then Miss Firth led them into the dining room of the Girls' Lodging House.

Long tables flanked by wooden benches filled the room. A line of girls snaked along the side wall, inching toward a serving counter. Each of them dropped a few coins in the till before taking a bowl of porridge with milk and bread.

Meg tried to back out of the line, not wanting to spend her coin.

Miss Firth put her hand on Meg's shoulder, urging her forward. "You needn't worry about paying for your breakfast this morning. The Children's Aid Society has arranged for that."

Meg felt a twinge of guilt as she ate more for breakfast than she and Mole had eaten for the last two days. Would they be feeding him too? She hadn't heard the Orphan's Asylum was any too generous with food. But it wouldn't help Mole for her to go hungry, so she pocketed a bit of bread for him and then tucked in.

After breakfast, and more washing up, Miss Firth gave each of the girls a new coat, a pair of shoes, and a name tag. By then it was nearly noon. Meg was exhausted and growing more anxious about Mole by the minute. He would be expecting her.

Miss Firth assured her that he would meet them on the ferry, but Meg didn't trust her. She wasn't going west without him! She'd jump off the ferry if he wasn't there.

They took a horse-drawn bus to the ferry. Miss Firth produced tickets, and they boarded the boat, making their way to the stern. To Meg's intense relief, Mole, almost unrecognizable in a new coat and clean face, broke free of a group of boys and ran to her.

"Hey, Meg. I thought you wasn't coming." He encircled her with his arms.

Meg shook loose of him. "Didn't I tell you I'd be coming? Careful now, or you'll get yourself all dirty again. Sure, I hardly knew it was you, you're so shiny."

"They wouldn't let me keep the coat we found, even though I told them you gave it to me. You ain't mad, are you? This one fits a lot better. And they let me keep the cap."

"Sure, I see that." Meg pulled it down over his eyes. "You're a regular gent now." The hard knot that had kept her stomach clenched the last two days loosened. She couldn't remember the last time he had been so happy.

The agent with the boys was a big man with a tidy beard and a brown bowler. "I'm Mr. Wills." He bowed slightly, then smiled at Miss Firth. The two of them settled into conversation.

The five boys with him lounged against the railing and looked even more ragged and wild than the girls did. Four of them were older than Meg, two nearly grown.

The whistle blew on the ferry and a big cloud of steam blew up. A huge engine below them rumbled. The giant paddle wheel started to turn, churning the water behind them into a white foam.

The children crowded against the railing, waving and shouting as they left the city behind. Meg stood back, watching. She didn't wave at anyone. She'd been born in New York, but it wasn't a place she would remember with any happiness. Ma and Da had built their dreams there and watched them die, then died with them. There was no one left there that Meg minded leaving.

But as she watched New York shrink away, her gut twisted. Bad as the last months had been, she knew the city's streets and alleys. She had no idea what might lie ahead

Suddenly a shout rang out. Two boys rolled on the deck, scratching and kicking each other. Mr. Wills pushed his way through the children ringing the fight. He dragged the boys apart and held them by their collars.

"That Danny Mills. He's a rotter, he is." The red-haired boy next to Meg shook his head. "Not even clear of the city, and already he's looking to get sent back."

"You're from Ireland." Meg recognized his brogue.

"What of it?" He clenched his fists, his blue eyes darkening.

Meg shrugged. "Nothing. Only that's where Ma and Da were from. County Cork."

The boy grinned. "Sorry. I guess I'm a mite touchy. Ma said it was on account of my red hair. I'm Sean McMahon." He stuck out his hand. "We left Ireland, County Clare, five months ago. We were six of us leaving. I'm the only one as made it here."

"Ship fever?" Meg remembered stories she'd heard of wretched immigrant ships.

Sean nodded. "The ship was almighty crowded, and the water was bad."

"That's hard," Meg said, but her words were wooden. What did she care about his troubles? She looked toward the boys who had been fighting. "Which one is Danny?" she asked, more to change the subject than out of any real interest.

"The biggest one, the blond. He's always picking fights. But he made a mistake here, and that's for sure. Buffalo is a match for him."

The second boy, Buffalo, was shorter than Danny, but stockier. He had lost his cap in the scuffle and his brown hair was wild. He kept his eyes locked on Danny and his fists tensed. Danny quit struggling against Mr. Wills and wiped his bloody lip on his sleeve. Looking at the fury in his eyes, Meg knew that fight wasn't over. She'd warn Mole to steer clear of him.

Suddenly Meg realized Mole wasn't beside her anymore. She jumped up and looked around frantically.

"If it's the little boy you're looking for," Sean said, "he's off playing with Tommy."

"Where?"

Sean pointed toward the front of the ferry, where the wealthier passengers sat or strolled about. "Don't be worrying. There's nowhere they can go off to."

But Meg didn't listen. She rushed forward to find him. Sean's words about Danny being sent back worried her. What if Mole were sent back? She would have to go too. That boy was fool enough to spoil everything.

Trying to be invisible, Meg slipped among the passengers at the bow of the ferry. No coils of rope littered the deck here. Finely dressed ladies and gents had benches to sit on and striped awnings to shield them from sun or rain. Little girls with shiny button-up shoes sat meekly by their mothers while their brothers in dapper waistcoats and knee-britches hung on the railing.

In spite of her new coat, Meg stood out. She couldn't hide her wild, unkempt hair or her ragged dress. She was still a street urchin, and they knew it. On all sides, people shrank away from her and stared.

She found Mole and Tommy leaning over the railing, munching on a couple of apples.

"Where did you get those?" Meg pulled them back from the railing and spun them toward her.

"Aw, Meg," Mole said. "I was hungry."

Tommy stared at her silently under his mop of black hair. His soft, dark eyes were wide with fear of her anger.

"Where did you get them?" Meg demanded again.

Mole drew a circle on the deck with his toe. "We took them from someone, I guess."

"They had so many," Tommy said. "We just took two. They won't miss them."

Meg shook Mole furiously. "I told you. We don't steal. Not ever!"

"But Meg, I was so hungry. They had plenty more."

Meg shook him again. "You'll get sent back to New York. No one will want you if you're a thief." No one will want me either, Meg realized. A watch was a lot more valuable than an apple. She clenched her teeth. No one would find out about that, not if she could help it.

Mole's eyes filled with tears. "You won't leave me, Meg, will you? I promise I won't never steal, never, ever again."

"Not much of a promise, is it, if you have to keep making it over. You're the one taking off here. I thought you couldn't stand to be out of my sight for two minutes. Did you forget about me just like that?"

Mole swiped at his eyes with his jacket sleeve. "I didn't forget you, Meg, honest. I was just playing."

She let go of his jacket and turned away. The boy was always playing and couldn't keep a thought in his head two minutes. "You stay down at our end of the boat where you belong. You get lost, no one will come looking for you."

Mole took her hand. "You will, Meg, won't you?"

Meg didn't answer. Without looking at him, she led the way past the shining benches and railing to the back of the boat where the street urchins sprawled about.

Mr. Wills and Miss Firth had brought along a picnic supper, which the children ate together in the stern of the boat, away from the other passengers.

"They think they're better than us." Danny spat in the direction of the wealthy passengers.

Arthur, a quiet boy Meg hadn't paid much attention to, shrugged. "Maybe they are," he muttered. Arthur was about Sean's height, but skinnier. He squinted all the time, like he had weak eyes. "They have more."

"That doesn't mean anything," Buffalo argued in a friendly way. "They're just luckier."

"I'd say we're pretty lucky." Dotty held Nan on her lap and helped to feed her. "A few days ago we had nothing better to do than beg in the streets. Now we've got food and a place to sleep, and we're heading to new homes, real homes."

"Luck's nothing," Danny said. "A fella takes what he wants, and if he ain't strong enough to do it, he dies." He slowed clenched his fist, as if to demonstrate. He had big hands, as rough and worn as a working man's.

Meg chewed her bread slowly. She didn't like Danny much, but he was right about luck. There wasn't any.

Night had settled in by the time they reached Albany. The ten children followed Miss Firth and Mr. Wills quietly from the dock to the station where they boarded a train. Inside the warm train carriage, it was hard to sit still. Meg squirmed on the backless wooden bench that served as a seat. Mole followed Tommy and Birdie as they ran up and down the aisle, dodging the trunks, satchels, and bundles of the various family groups sharing their car.

Finally, the train whistle blew a loud, shrill blast. The children jumped up, crowding around the door. The train began to move with a jerk that sent them all sprawling. Meg untangled herself and dragged Mole out of the heap.

"Sit down, everyone." Miss Firth passed out bread and cheese for a light supper. After eating, the children crowded the windows, but it had grown too dark to see anything.

"Get some sleep now." Mr. Wills blew out the kerosene lamps lighting the car.

Meg and Mole curled up together on one bench but Mole kept bobbing up to look out the window again.

"Stop fidgeting," Meg told Mole. Behind her, she heard Dotty singing a lullaby to Nan. Across the aisle, Sean pulled his cap down over his red hair and settled into the corner to doze, while Buffalo and

Arthur talked quietly. In the seat opposite, Tommy and Birdie argued about how fast they were going, their voices getting louder and louder until Mr. Wills separated them.

Danny sat alone, at the far end of the car.

Gradually, the voices died down. Mole fell asleep beside her. Meg stayed awake, listening to the rhythmic clacking of the wheels, like a new voice, talking just to her. She couldn't quite decide if it said, 'New life, new life, new life' or 'Go back! Go back! Go back!'

CHAPTER 7: SO MANY TREES!

Meg woke early the next morning to the clacking of the wheels along the rail. The warmth of the car and Mole's small body curled up beside her wrapped around her like a soft blanket. She didn't want to open her eyes. But Mole's head leaning on her arm had put it to sleep. She eased her arm out from under him, so as not to wake him. Pins and needles shot up and down it. Gingerly rubbing her arm, she looked around the dim interior of the train car.

The other children were all still sleeping, sprawled out on the wooden benches pushed together to make beds. Meg groaned softly and stretched her neck. She was stiff all over from sitting up all night. She rolled her shoulders and gazed out the window.

The sun, just coming up behind the train, cast an odd, pinkish light to the countryside. Meg forgot her stiffness as she stared in awe at the fairyland rolling out before her. Never had she seen so much empty space. Trees, grass, and fields of drying corn spread out on all sides. Farmhouses cropped up here and there, along with vast tracts of open, uncultivated land in between.

Meg glanced at the sleeping forms in the car, then slipped Jake's watch out of her pocket. The weight of it in the palm of her hand was a comfort, a sort of insurance against her troubles. A small thing really, to send them fleeing across such a big country. Then she felt a shadow over her. She looked up, automatically closing her hand over the watch.

But Danny had seen it. He didn't say a word, standing there, but she knew. His eyes glittered with greed. Meg felt a shiver all the way down to her toes.

"Glory be!" said Dotty from the seat behind Meg. "Would you look at all them trees!"

Danny moved on past Meg's seat, and she slipped the watch back into her pocket.

The other children woke, and a chorus of oh's and ah's broke the silence. Trees of every color, from deepest green, to orange and red as brilliant as fire, to a dark, rich purple, lined the tracks and spread out on either side.

Meg shook off thoughts of Danny. So what if he knew about the watch? It wasn't like he would tattle on her, and as long as she stayed with the group, he wouldn't have a chance to take it from her.

"Welcome to Ohio." Mr. Wills handed Arthur a sack of bread and Sean a pitcher of milk and a dipper. "Pass these around."

Mole blinked his eyes sleepily when Meg woke him, then pulled his knees up to his chest and leaned back against the wall of the car. "I'm not hungry, Meg." He closed his eyes again.

"Go on with you!" Meg shook him. "You're always hungry."

Mole shook his head slightly, pulled his knees up tighter, and didn't answer.

Meg shook him harder. "You have to eat something." She tore off a bite of bread, dipped it in the milk, and pushed it into his mouth. Mole chewed and swallowed without protest and without opening his eyes. Meg brushed her hand against his cheek and felt the unnatural heat from fever. She tore another bite of bread and fed it to him. In this way he ate his share of the bread, and only then did Meg let him go back to sleep.

When Mole woke again an hour later, he looked a bit better. Although his eyes were still too bright and his cheeks flushed, he sat up and looked out the window with interest. Soon, he and Tommy had a contest going to see who could see the most cows. Since neither boy could count past twenty, they kept having to start over.

Meg breathed a silent sigh of relief. No need to keep fretting if Mole was up to playing.

The train stopped shortly before noon at a small town past

Cleveland. Mole took the scrunched up brown cap out of his pocket and put it on.

"Is this where our new parents will be?" Tommy asked.

"No. This is only our lunch break. We have almost one hour here." Miss Firth clapped her hands. "Children, we must stay together here. The train won't wait for us."

She and Mr. Wills herded the children off the train, across a narrow dirt road, and into a small restaurant for lunch. The building was made out of clean, smooth pine boards and had two large glass windows looking out the front. Red checked curtains, drawn back with black ribbon, hung in each window. A half dozen tables filled the room, each one covered with a matching red gingham cloth. Meg rubbed her hands on her skirt, then ran a finger across the smooth cloth before sitting down.

It didn't take Meg long to finish the meat and potatoes on her plate, but Mole only picked at his. He leaned his head on his elbow and pushed the food into little mounds. Meg snatched the fork from him and stabbed a potato. "Eat this," she insisted.

Mole swallowed dutifully a few bites and then turned his face away. "I can't eat any more."

Meg looked around quickly, then switched plates with him and ate his share. She worried that if Mr. Wills or Miss Firth saw he wasn't eating, they would figure out he was sick and send him back.

They gathered in front of the restaurant to return to the train. Miss Firth counted noses. "Has anyone seen Birdie? I told you all we had to stay together."

No one had seen her since entering the restaurant.

"All of you bigger children, spread out and look for her," Mr. Wills ordered. "I'll see if I can delay the train. Hurry."

Meg stomped back down the street away from the train. She kicked a rock out of her path, then swore at the pain in her toes. Birdie knew she should be back. What if the train went on without them? They would all be stuck here, in the middle of nowhere. All because of a rotten, foul-mouthed beggar. Meg was so angry she almost didn't hear the soft sobbing coming from the end of the alley beside the restaurant.

There, hiding among the boxes and barrels of garbage, was Birdie, her arms and legs curled around her skinny body.

Startled out of her anger, Meg walked up and touched her shoulder. She would never have pegged Birdie as a crier.

Birdie jerked away at her touch, as if she'd been burned. "Leave me alone." Birdie's eyes flashed angrily.

Meg drew back her hand and straightened. "Hurry up. Don't you know everyone's waiting on you?"

"Let them wait," Birdie said. "Or go without me. What do I care?"

Meg frowned at her. The little brat couldn't make them all lose out, not if Meg Kelly had anything to say about it! She grabbed Birdie's hand and jerked her up out of the trash heap.

"You may not give a sow's ear for any of the rest of us, but there's those that do," Meg said.

Birdie was strong for her size, but skinny. Meg kept an tight grip on her wrist as she dragged the younger girl back toward the train.

"Whatever were you thinking, child?" Miss Firth scolded as she hurried them aboard. She thanked Meg over and over again.

Meg felt her cheeks going red. She hadn't done anything. She would have left the girl if she could.

Even before Miss Firth was through talking, Mole squeezed up beside her and hung on her hand. He glared at Birdie when she sat on the other side of Meg. Then he squirmed even closer.

Meg pushed at him. "Shove over," she said crossly. "You don't have to be sitting on top of me, you hear?"

By evening the monotonous clacking of the wheels on the rails almost hypnotized her. Mole dozed with his head in her lap, and Birdie leaned against her on the other side. Meg felt suffocated between the two of them, but another part of her was gratified by the younger children's attention. She tried to ignore both feelings. She could take care of Mole, all right, but it wouldn't do her or Birdie any good to get attached. Finally, Meg's eyelids drooped, and she dozed along with the others.

As the sky darkened, the children pushed the benches close together into makeshift beds. They spread out the straw mattresses that Mr. Wills had purchased in town.

Sean helped her with the one for her and Mole, then sat beside her. "Is your brother still sick?"

"He's not sick," she snapped. "No one said he's sick."

"Sorry." Sean spread his hands wide in apology. "I didn't mean to rile you. I was just asking."

"Just don't go saying he's sick. Mole is fine."

They sat silently for a few minutes. Meg wished she hadn't been so short with him. He'd never believe her now. But it was true. Mole wasn't really sick. He would be fine in the morning.

"What made you leave New York?" Sean asked after a short silence.

"I didn't know what else to do," Meg said. That was true enough. She didn't have to tell him about the watch. "Da died six years ago and now Ma's dead too. Nothing there for us now."

Sean nodded. "I guess that's why we left Ireland. The land was all used up. Da hoped to come out here and start a new farm. I never thought I'd be here without him."

Miss Firth blew out the lanterns, and everyone settled down to sleep.

Even Mole woke early the next morning. Meg studied him and fretted. He was still pale, but the dark circles under his eyes seemed lighter. He hadn't coughed too much in the night.

They ate bread and milk for breakfast again. Mole didn't touch his bread, but Meg decided it was because he was excited, not because he was sick.

Miss Firth insisted each one wash hands, face and neck. She passed a comb around. Meg helped Mole and then Birdie too, when the little girl asked her. Dotty fixed little Nan up so her face shone.

The children crowded around the windows as the train slowed and pulled into a town in western Indiana. Although nothing like New York, this town was bigger than any of the places they had stopped the day before to take on wood and water for the steam engine. The train chugged past a stable, three stores, and two taverns. Rows of neat, two-story board houses lined the streets. These houses were smaller than the tenement houses of New York, but newer. There was nothing crooked, rickety or ragged. Clearly, Meg and Mole didn't belong here.

The children scrambled off the train as soon as it stopped. Mr.

Wills stood at the head of the group and warned them sternly to stay together.

Miss Firth made sure the mattresses were stored safely in the stationhouse, and nothing was left on the train. They were scheduled to spend the night here and catch a different train tomorrow.

Mole hung on Meg's hand and leaned against her.

"Pastor Brown should have been here to meet us," Mr. Wills muttered. He looked up from his notebook and scanned the street in both directions. A few horses stood tied in front of stores. He closed the notebook with a snap. "No matter. We shall simply walk to the church and meet him." Looking straight up the street from the train station, Meg could see a tall, whitewashed church. Mr. Wills led the way toward it.

Suddenly a raucous crowd of men pushed out of the tavern closest to the train station.

"Go back where you came from," one of them called out.

"We don't want city scum in our town," another yelled.

Mr. Wills straightened his back and marched on. Danny glared at everyone around him. He looked ready to pick up a rock and prove just what city scum could do. Mr. Wills kept his hand on the boy's shoulder, and Meg kept a tight grip on Mole's hand.

She should have known this promise was nothing but a dream. They'd never find places here, nor anywhere else. These people were no different from the angry footman in New York who had run her off and the rich lady she had seen climbing into her carriage. No one cared about them.

The men heckled them all the way down Main Street to the door of the church. "Pay them no mind, children," Miss Firth said. "There is rifftaff in all parts of the world."

The minister met them at the church. A small, round man, he rubbed his hands together nervously. "I'm sorry I was unable to meet the train," he said. "Come in." He closed the door behind them.

"You are Pastor Brown?" Mr. Wills consulted his notebook again.

"Yes, yes." The minister nodded, jerking his head up and down like a puppet on a string.

"Where are the families you contacted? In your letter you stated three families want children."

Pastor Brown's eyes shifted nervously from Mr. Wills to Miss Firth and back. He carefully avoided looking at the children. "Well." He coughed and began again. "Well, it seems they have changed their minds. I'm sorry."

"All of them?" Mr. Wills' voice held a note of disbelief.

"Well, yes." Pastor Brown looked at the floor. "It seems some of the townsfolk object to the city children living here. They ... um ... were quite ... um ... strong in their denouncements. I'm afraid they have managed to convince the others."

"What do you intend to do?" Mr. Wills folded his arms across his chest and glared at the shorter man. "Do you expect us to sleep in the street? There's not another train until tomorrow."

"Well, the missus said we would put you up tonight. It'll be a squeeze, but I suppose we can manage." He laughed nervously.

Mr. Wills gathered the children around him. "There has been a mistake, but we have other towns on our route, and we'll go on. Don't give up hope." He looked at each child in turn, but Meg could see no one believed him. And why should they? She knew promises weren't worth anything.

"Stay in the yard here, close to the church today," Mr. Wills instructed. "Play quietly, and stay away from the townsfolk."

Meg sat with her back against the church in sunshine too weak to warm her. Danny squatted near her.

"You got the time?" he asked quietly.

Meg shook her head without looking at him.

"Well, imagine that. A fine timepiece like that and you don't know what time it is! Maybe I can help you fix it. Why don't you let me take a look?" His voice was very soft, but the threat in it was clear. Meg edged further away.

Out the corner of her eye, she saw Mole chasing Tommy across the yard. Halfway to the fence, he doubled over, coughing. Meg jumped up.

"I've got to help my brother." She ran over to Mole to pound him on the back. She didn't look back at Danny, but she could feel him watching her.

At noon, Mrs. Brown called them inside. All four adults and

the ten children crowded around her table. The kitchen was so small Meg had to scrunch her shoulders and squeeze her knees together to fit between Mole and Sean on a bench against the wall. Nan sat on Dotty's lap, and the other boys stood at the table corners since there weren't enough chairs.

Mrs. Brown bustled around the table. A thin woman with large hands and a permanent frown, she never sat down. She plopped mounded spoonfuls of beans on any empty plate as if the sight of it offended her.

She's got no right to be mad at us, Meg thought. The children hadn't asked for this kind of welcome.

Pastor Brown muttered a polite request for more cornbread.

His wife scowled at him and nearly threw the smallest piece left onto his plate.

So it was her husband she was mad at, Meg realized, not the children. It served him right, not that it made any difference.

After lunch Nan took a nap, but the others went back outside. Birdie, Mole, and Tommy played crack the whip.

"There's always more towns." Dotty sat beside Meg against the church and drew a design in the dust with a small stick.

"What's to say they'll be any different?" Meg demanded. "Who in this whole country is going to want us?"

Dotty rubbed out her picture and started over. "A person has to believe. With a little luck, there will be homes for all of us."

"There's no such thing as luck!" Meg stood up angrily and walked away. Dotty was stupid, believing in anything. Meg didn't have to listen to her.

After supper, Mrs. Brown pounded on the piano for awhile. Meg felt herself dozing as she listened. Her head fell forward. With a start, she jerked awake. Her heart raced in sudden panic.

But nothing had changed. Mole lay sleeping in her lap. The other children sprawled on the floor.

All except Danny. From across the room, he watched her. His eyes were half closed, but that didn't fool her. She shuddered.

Finally, Mrs. Brown stood up and closed the piano. "Time for bed," she announced. She scooped Nan up. "We'll take the little one upstairs." She glared at Pastor Brown, daring him to argue, but he only looked at the floor and fiddled with his vest button. "Boys sleep in the kitchen, girls in the parlor," Mrs. Brown continued. "Miss Firth, you may use the spare bedroom."

Mr. Wills hustled the boys into the kitchen with an armload of blankets. "You too," he said to Mole who clung to Meg's skirt.

Mole looked up at Meg with wide, frightened eyes.

"Go on with you." Meg pushed him away. "Don't be such a crybaby."

"Please, Meg?" He mouthed the words. "She gets to sleep in there with you." He pointed at Birdie.

Meg shook her head. "I'm only going to be in the next room. Go on."

Mr. Wills took his hand and led him away. Mole looked over his shoulder toward Meg. She turned away.

The girls spread the blankets on the floor and put out the lights, but Meg couldn't sleep. She could hear Mole coughing and sniffling in the next room. He always made it so hard. She wasn't leaving him, was she?

Meg imagined herself back in New York in the tiny, stuffy room with Ma. It hadn't been so bad, at least before Jake came. The hard knot in her stomach tightened. Why had Ma let him stay? She should have kicked him out. It was all Ma's fault, all of it. She had let Da go and Jake stay. She had turned to drink and stumbled in front of an ice wagon. She could have done different. She could have taken care of them.

Meg clenched the blanket as anger washed over her. But was she any better? She was a thief, and here she was, speaking bad of the dead, or least ways thinking it. And her last words to Ma had been angry and hurtful. Meg's breath caught in her throat like a huge stone lodged there, aching. She was nothing but a monster, who drove away her own mother. Meg groaned and hugged the blanket around her ears. She drew a long, shuddering breath. She wouldn't cry. Not here. Not now. It was too late for any of that now.

A muffled sob next to her broke in on her thoughts. Meg reached out her hand automatically, before she remembered Mole was in the kitchen. "Birdie?"

Birdie sniffed. "What?"

"Nothing," Meg answered, but she found Birdie's hand under

her blanket and held onto it. There was no need for words.

Next morning, all the children woke early. Mrs. Brown looked like a different person, smiling and humming as she ladled thick, creamy oatmeal into their bowls.

Meg narrowed her eyes. What had happened overnight to change the woman's attitude so much?

As soon as everyone was served, Mrs. Brown clapped her handa and announced, "We've decided to keep Little Nan. Our town has promised to provide homes for three. We can't keep that promise, but we'll do our share."

"Very good," Miss Firth said. "I'll get the papers ready as soon as we've eaten."

Mr. Wills shook hands with the Browns and promised to be in touch.

Finally, it was time to leave for the train station. Dotty cried as she hugged Nan one last time.

"Dotty should never have let herself get so caught up with the little girl," Meg told Sean as they settled down in their seats on the next train. "It's easier if you don't care."

"I don't know about that," Sean said softly. "Danny doesn't care about anyone but himself. I wouldn't want to be like him."

Meg didn't have an answer for that.

The train whistle blew. With gathering speed, the train pulled out of town. Mole sat very close to Meg and leaned his head on her shoulder. He was quiet for so long, Meg thought he had fallen asleep. When he spoke, his voice barely above a whisper, it startled her.

"There's no houses, Meg," he said. "Just so many trees. I'm scared of the woods."

"Hush." Meg smoothed down his tangled hair. "Don't you be worrying."

Too bad she couldn't follow her own advice.

CHAPTER 8: WHAT'S LEFT NOW?

The next morning Miss Firth put her hand on Mole's forehead. "Is he getting worse?"

"He's fine," Meg insisted. "It's just the dust on the train making him cough."

Miss Firth pursed her lips and shook her head. She said nothing more, at least not to Meg.

But as Meg watched, Miss Firth went over to Mr. Wills, bent and whispered something to him, then nodded in her direction. Meg wrapped her arm around Mole. They weren't going back, no matter what. They couldn't.

Birdie came and sat beside her. "Dotty showed me a new cat's cradle. Want to play?"

Mole grabbed Meg's hand. "Play with me, not her."

"What's gotten into you?" Meg slapped his hand away and scowled at Birdie. "I'm not playing with either of you."

Four hours later, Mr. Wills announced the train would stop for lunch in ten minutes. By then, Mole was napping with his head in her lap. Meg roused him.

He followed her sleepily, but stopped at the steps. "My cap," he cried and darted back for it.

"It's just a rag from the junk heap," Meg scolded. "Nothing to get so riled over."

Mole pulled it down over his eyes without answering.

Lunch was served in small, dusty tavern with bare tables and a splintery wood floor. Dingy yellow curtains drooped in the windows, doing little to cheer the room.

With only half an hour to eat, Meg gobbled down the beef stew in front of her, urging Mole to try his. He only pushed it back and forth on his plate.

"You've got to eat," she hissed at him. She grabbed his spoon and shoved it into his mouth, feeding him like she had when he was small. Mole chewed and swallowed obediently.

He hadn't even finished half of it when Mr. Wills shouted for them to reboard the train. Meg shoved another bite of food at Mole, then grabbed his arm to hurry him along. The train didn't wait for stragglers.

Danny, still sitting at a table near the door, stuck out his leg in front of Mole. Mole went sprawling, and his cap fell out of his pocket. He scrambled after it, but Danny picked it up and held it just out of reach.

"Give it back," Mole shouted, flailing at Danny.

He laughed, holding the little boy off with one hand.

Meg grabbed Mole's collar and jerked him back to safety. She shoved him behind her and squared off in front of Danny. "You're too old to be teasing a little kid. What do you want with a rag like that?"

"It's my bargaining chip," Danny said, still grinning. "You've got something a lot more valuable that I want. Give it to me, and I'll give the kid back his rag."

Meg felt the weight of the watch in her pocket. She resisted the urge to wrap her hand around it. The cap wasn't worth it. "I've got nothing for you." She spun away from him and dragged Mole along.

"Meg," he wailed, pulling to get free of her, but she didn't relax her hold on him until they were safely back on board the train.

Meg pushed him onto the bench and sat down beside him.

Mole scrunched away from her as close to the wall as he could get. "You let him steal my cap," he said forlornly. "The one you gave me."

"Sure, and what was I supposed to do?" Meg snapped at him. "Let him break my arm, me trying to grab it back?"

Mole turned his back toward her without speaking.

Danny boarded the train just as it was pulling away from the station. Very deliberately, he sat down on the bench in front of Meg and Mole. He dangled the cap out the window. It flapped in the breeze "Want it?"

Mole sat forward. "Yes, please."

"Too bad for you," Danny sneered. He let go of the cap. The wind swirled it away.

Meg grabbed for Mole as he tried to dive out the window after it. "It's just a stupid rag," she said angrily.

"You could have saved it." Mole buried his face in his arm and cried silently.

Danny leaned close to Meg. "I always get what I want," he whispered.

Meg shivered in spite of herself. She patted Mole's back while he cried, but he didn't respond.

Gradually his shoulders stopped shaking, and he relaxed into sleep. Meg remained alert, questions chasing each other round and round in her head. What would Danny do? The worst of it was Mole was right, in a way. She could have traded the watch for the cap. But would that really have helped?

Meg stared out the window as the train sped past cornfields and apple orchards. The clacking wheels kept asking, "What now? What now? What now?"

As evening approached, the train pulled into Clarksford, the second scheduled stop where families wanted children. Meg hung back as the other children crowded around the door, and the train chugged to a stop. The brakes screeched and the engine let out a whoosh of steam.

Mr. Buchwald, the town minister, stood on the platform to greet them before the train had completely stopped. He towered above everyone else on the platform, but he bent over to shake hands with each child.

Mole hung on Meg's skirt. When Meg pushed him forward, his fingers barely touched those of the minister before he jerked his hand away.

The minister smiled at them through a thick, graying beard. His hair was wild, as wild as Da's had been. Mr. Buchwald ran his fingers through his hair so it stood on end, just like Da had always done.

But when Mr. Buchwald smiled at Meg, she frowned. He couldn't fool her. Just because he looked like Da didn't mean she had to trust him After all, Da had run out on them.

"Mr. Buchwald has a surprise for us at the schoolhouse," Mr. Wills told them. "Let's show him what ladies and gentlemen we can all be."

Meg's scowl deepened. Ladies and gentlemen? Not hardly. They started off in a ragged line as Mr. Buchwald led the way. Meg stood still on the train platform, studying the smooth worn planks. Traveling wasn't so bad. She could just go on and on. No sense in getting hopeful.

Miss Firth put her hand on Meg's shoulder and gently pushed her forward. Meg shrugged free of the hand, but followed the others into the schoolhouse. Mole clung to her skirt.

Inside, forty or more people jammed together, all talking and laughing. Meg pulled her shawl tighter in spite of the warmth. In New York, strangers ignored each other. All these strangers stared at the children, smiled at them and talked to them, expecting answers.

Meg reached for Mole's hand. Keeping her head down, she slipped through the crowd. She led Mole to the benches set up in front of the schoolroom for the children. Mole fidgeted, swinging his legs, until Meg nudged him and told him to sit still.

One by one, the other children sat down. Mr. Buchwald joined them. He squeezed Sean's shoulder and smiled at Dotty. Then he faced the crowd and cleared his throat. His voice was rich and deep, an easy voice to listen to.

"I want to welcome you, one and all, most especially our new friends from far away. Some of us are more than a little nervous." He smiled at the children. "So we'll eat first and then get down to business after we've had a chance to get to know one another. Good food makes good friends. We've got plenty of food, so let's eat and get on with the friend making."

In the second room of the schoolhouse, there was a table set up with all kinds of foods, many that Meg had never seen before.

She wasn't hungry. Her stomach was too tight. She led Mole around the table and helped him get food. He wasn't anxious to try anything, but Meg kept piling on scoops of this salad or that stew until his plate was piled so full he would never finish it in a week.

Meg pulled him away from the table. They sat in the corner to eat. Mole still had not spoken, but he slowly chewed and swallowed as she put each bite in his mouth.

By the time supper was over, and several kerosene lamps had been lit to drive off the gathering night, most of the children were comfortable enough to visit with the townsfolk, answering questions.

Meg nudged Mole. "Go on over there. Say hello to someone."

For an answer he just wrapped his arms around his knees.

"Fine one I am to be ordering you about," Meg muttered to herself. No one would ever pick them if she couldn't even talk to the people here, but her tongue felt like mush filling her whole mouth.

Meg sat for what seemed like ages. Her leg went to sleep and when she moved it, pins and needles shot up and down her whole leg. She shifted, wiggling her toes until the tingling stopped.

Mole hadn't moved since they sat down. With the heat of his body against her and the warmth of the crowded schoolroom, Meg felt suffocated.

Meg took off her old shawl and set it beside Mole. "I'll be right back," she told him. "Don't get yourself in any trouble."

Mole didn't answer.

Meg slipped out the back door to look for the outhouse. Bright stars lay scattered across the dark, moonless sky as if they had been carelessly thrown away. The highest branches of several tall trees swished back and forth overhead. Meg hunched her shoulders against the cold wind, wishing she had brought her shawl. She set off across the playground toward the small building at the edge of the clearing.

She didn't see the dark shape in the shadows behind the door until it rose and grabbed her. Before she could scream, an arm as hard as Jake's wrapped around her, and a rough, work-worn hand clamped over her mouth.

She knew at once it was Danny. She was no match for him, but she struggled anyway, trying to hit him, kick him, anything to get free. He held her as easily as he had Mole, ignoring those few blows she managed to land.

"I need that watch more than you do." He thrust his free hand into her pocket.

Meg tried to bite him, but Danny's hand squeezed her jaw too tightly. He reached the watch, pulled it free of her pocket and flung her away from him in one smooth gesture.

She fell sideways, her shoulder hitting the ground first, then her head. By the time she sat up, Danny was gone.

Meg held her head with both hands, too dizzy to see straight. She drew a long, shuddering breath that was more than half sob. Slowly she stood up on legs that wouldn't stop trembling and straightened her skirt and apron. She went on to the outhouse and sat, trying to steady her breath. Finally she went back inside the schoolhouse.

She was better off without the watch, Meg told herself. It was no pot of gold. It hadn't brought her any kind of luck.

But it had brought her way out west, Meg knew, and what was she to do out here with no insurance? Her pocket felt very empty.

Mole sat exactly as she had left him, hunched over with his back to her as if nothing had happened. Meg wanted to shake him, to scream at him. What right had he to sulk over a ragged cap when she had lost the only thing of real value they had? But she couldn't tell him about the watch. Lips pressed together, Meg slid down the wall to sit leaning against it. She forced her breath to slow down, but her hands shook, and her legs still trembled.

When her breathing finally returned to normal, Meg looked up at the crowd in the room and saw that the choosing was just about finished. Most people had taken their leave. The remaining folk had formed new family groups including some of the children from New York.

The adults took some time to fill out all the agreement papers and sign the necessary documents. Dotty had been picked by a family with five young children. She already had the youngest one in her lap, bouncing him up and down on her knee. She smiled at the woman who would be her new mother and at all her new brothers and sisters. Meg snorted. Dotty looked happy there, but Dotty could smile at a shack with a leaky roof.

Josephine, Arthur, and Tommy had been chosen too. Tommy shook hands with Mole as he said good-bye.

Mole slipped his hand into Meg's as he watched them leave. "My cap and my friend gone." He sniffled. "You won't leave me, Meg, will you?"

"Didn't I say it, about a hundred times?" She brushed the hair out of his eyes, her fingers lingering a moment on his brow. Was it still just as feverishly hot? Or was the heat she felt there coming from the overheated room? She couldn't tell anymore.

Gradually the crowd in the schoolhouse thinned until Mr. Buchwald, Mr. Wills, Miss Firth, Meg, Mole, Sean, Buffalo and Birdie were the only ones left. Meg felt a surprising stab of loneliness. She hadn't cared about any of the others, not really, but she had grown used to them. She ought to know by now everyone left eventually.

Mr. Wills directed the children to straighten the chairs and sweep the schoolroom. He shook hands with Mr. Buchwald and thanked him. "I can't think what has happened to Danny." Mr. Wills said. "I fear he's up to some mischief."

"Don't worry about that," Mr. Buchwald said. "The boy will turn up somewhere."

"You should have just given him what he wanted first off," Mole told Meg mournfully as he held a dustpan for her. "Least ways then I'd have my cap still."

Meg stiffened. Did he know about the watch? He couldn't have seen it, could he? He must be blathering on about nothing. In any case, what did it matter, now it was gone? She pulled her hand loose from his. "Can't you just shut up about that stupid cap?"

The children slept in the schoolhouse that night. It was cold, and they crowded together for warmth.

Meg thought she must be getting soft. The room was nowhere near as cold as the streets. She fell asleep with Mole hanging on one hand and Birdie the other.

The next morning Danny was still gone. They searched for him, but no one really expected to find him. They decided they had seen the last of Dan Mill.

"Imagine him wanting to go back to the life he led." Mr. Wills frowned. "No honest work, no place to rest his head."

"Yes, well," Mr. Buchwald shook his head as if he really cared about Dan Mill's fate. "I always say, you can lead a horse to water, but you can't make him drink."

"True, Mr. Buchwald, too true. But I can't help wondering how he'll manage going back."

Meg knew. Her watch would more than pay for a ticket. Could be they were better off since he had stolen the watch. She could stop fretting about it, like she had told Mole about his stupid cap. But she felt lost without the weight of it in her pocket and the solid promise it had given.

A small, quiet group of children boarded the train later that same afternoon. Mole squeezed up close to Meg on the seat, even though there was plenty of room, and the car wasn't cold. Birdie slid in beside her.

Meg sighed, but she didn't push either of them away.

CHAPTER 9: A WARM BED AND ENOUGH TO EAT

As Meg woke up to the clacking of the wheels on the rails the next morning, it seemed to her they had always been riding on a train, on and on forever, with no beginning and no end. The wheels which always seemed to talk to her now were saying, "No place, no place, no place."

Meg took the bread that Miss Firth passed out. She ate without talking to anyone. Mole wouldn't eat, even when she tried to feed him. Meg ate his portion so no one would notice.

In the seat behind her, Sean and Buffalo played with a deck of battered cards. "Do you think they'll be happy back there?" Sean asked as he dealt the next hand.

"They would be dumb not to be," Buffalo said. "At least they'll have enough to eat and a place to sleep."

"Are you supposing there will be homes for the lot of us?" Sean continued. "I've no mind to go back to New York."

"I won't go back," Buffalo insisted. "I'd run off first and stay on out here. I lived on my own in New York. I guess I can take care of myself just as well anywhere else."

"Well, I'll not be going back either," Sean declared. "My Da said we'd try our hands out west and I mean to do it. Could be, I'll go all the way to California."

Buffalo grinned and punched his shoulder. "Sure, you go on

out there and make us all rich on gold."

"No," Sean said. "Not gold to make us rich--farming! All those gold miners will be wanting to eat, won't they?"

They both laughed. Meg closed her eyes. Fine plans they had, but not for her. She'd find no place out here on her own, with none to sell to or beg from. And Mole, hanging on her for years yet, too young and too small to be helping. Worst of all, they had no reason to be here and no way out now the watch was gone.

After lunch, Mole scooted across the aisle to play cat's cradle with Birdie. Meg stared out the window, trying not to think of anything. Not Mole, not Ma, not Da, not New York ... and especially not what might lie ahead.

Suddenly, a shriek from Mole roused her. Birdie yanked on a fistful of Mole's hair while he punched her in the stomach.

Meg grabbed both of them by the collars and pulled them apart. She plopped Birdie down in the seat and kept a tight grip on Mole. "You want to get sent back, the pair of you? It's no good fighting like that!"

"They won't take you away from me, will they?" Mole glared past Meg at Birdie. "If someone wants just you and not me, you won't make me go back to New York, will you?"

"No," Meg said. She wiped his tears on her skirt. "I told you and told you we'll stay together. If one of us gets sent back, we'll both go." She glared at Birdie. "And don't be listening to anyone telling you different."

Birdie stuck out her tongue at Meg. "I got taken from my sister. She got sent to Blackwell's, and there weren't nothing either of us could do to stop them. You don't know so much."

"Will they do that to us, Meg?" Mole asked. "Are you going to Blackwell's?"

Meg scowled. What did he know about the prison? "I'm not going to Blackwell's and neither are you," she told Mole with as much conviction as she could. It was true, wasn't it? You couldn't get thrown in prison for stealing a watch you didn't have, could you? Meg shoved Mole into the seat by the window. "You just hush. You ought to listen to me, what's always taken care of you, not her." Meg turned her back on Birdie.

Eventually, Mole dozed again with his head in her lap. He was sleeping when the train crossed the Mississippi River. His forehead felt hot and dry under Meg's hand. His breathing sounded raspy. Meg rubbed his back gently.

The train ran along the river for an hour, then slowed as it neared the next scheduled stop, a small river town in Minnesota.

"Now remember," Miss Firth told them, "even if we don't find places for all of you here, we have two more towns on the list. No one will have to go back to New York."

They washed their hands and faces with cold water, leaning over the back rail of the car. Meg combed her hair and then helped Mole with his. Fine soot from the train stained their clothes, but they brushed out the wrinkles as best they could. Meg's stomach tightened in spite of Miss Firth's assurances. She looked out the window.

Beside them, the river rolled gently between high bluffs, higher than the tenement houses in New York. The train slowed to go around a bend. Then suddenly in front of them was the town. Smooth, plank houses stood in neat rows along a wide, dirt road. A few ramshackle cabins with old, graying wood clung to the edges of town, but most buildings were new, made of bright, yellow pine.

The brakes screeched, and the clacking wheels slowed. The train rolled to a stop. Meg wiped her sweaty palms on her skirt. She smoothed down Mole's hair once more. Then she took his hand and followed the others down the narrow steps to the platform.

The man who met them at the station was clean shaven, with clear, blue eyes, and a quiet air of peace. "I'm Reverend Aleer." He shook hands with Mr. Wills and Miss Firth, then with each one of the children. "We were expecting you yesterday."

"We were delayed by express trains going through," Mr. Wills explained.

"The families I wrote you about are farmers. They will come back into town this evening." Reverend Aleer pulled out his pocket watch and peered at it. "We have several hours. Why not stretch your legs a bit? See the town. Meet at the church for supper. Folks will be bringing potluck."

"Thank you, Reverend." Miss Firth nodded. "That's a fine idea. I'm sure we could all do with a bit of fresh air after the train. All right, children. Stay in pairs, don't wander off too far, and don't be late."

Buffalo and Sean shoved their hands in their pockets. They sauntered off, whistling.

Birdie looked ready to skip after them, but Miss Firth caught her by the hand. "You'll stay with me, Miss. I'm not about to lose you again."

Before Meg could decide what to do, Mole pulled at her skirt. "I'm cold." He was shivering even to make his teeth chatter. "I want to sit down." He coughed weakly.

Meg put her shawl around him. "You can't sit here on the street." She looked around.

Miss Firth was arguing with Birdie, and Mr. Wills had gone after the boys.

"We'll go inside the church." Half supporting, half dragging him, she led him into the stone church near the school house. They sat in the shadows near the back. Meg wished she could tell someone about Mole. She felt so helpless.

But if she told anyone Mole was sick, she feared they would be sent back to New York. After all, no one wanted sick children. And if that happened, Mole would die. Meg couldn't fool herself about that. She would just have to take care of Mole. She always had. He would be all right as soon as he got used to being warm and having enough to eat. He had to be.

Mole dozed restlessly in her lap while they waited. At one point, Meg left him to bring back a drink of water. Every half hour or so, she stepped to the back of the church and peered outside to judge the time.

Finally the sun began to set. Mole seemed better after his long nap. His cheeks weren't so flushed, and he wasn't coughing so much. Meg took his hand and led him to the meeting hall beside the sanctuary.

A small crowd gathered as the others returned. The people laughed and talked among themselves like old friends, but to Meg they seemed a jumble of foreign faces. Bearded men clomped across the wooden floor in heavy work boots. They had big hands and loud voices. Their wives, dressed in dark calicoes sprigged with flowers, chattered like a flock of pigeons squabbling over crumbs.

Meg perched on the edge of the hardwood chair and gripped Mole's hand. Whether it was to keep him close by or to comfort him, she didn't know. Looking at the milling crowd made her dizzy, so she stared at the bare plank boards of the floor.

She saw the feet first. Small, plump feet in black, high button shoes. A woman's feet.

"I am Mrs. Stein. You are one of the orphans?" The woman spoke with a heavy German accent.

Meg looked up. Small and plump, like her feet, the woman stood in front of Meg. Soft brown hair was twisted into a bun at the back of her head. Stray wisps of it escaped and floated around her face like cobwebs. Meg realized Mrs. Stein was waiting for an answer. She nodded silently.

"Me too." Mole's eyes shone with fever. "I'm with her. We're together." Meg nudged him into silence.

"Your brother?" Mrs. Stein asked Meg.

Again Meg nodded. Her tongue felt thick and dry. She couldn't find any words. If she didn't speak, would Mrs. Stein just walk away?

"Hugo, come here," Mrs. Stein called. She turned to Meg. "That is my husband, Mr. Stein."

A huge blond man came over, followed by a parade of small boys who could only be his sons. "Yes, Anna?" he said.

"This is the girl we want," Mrs. Stein said.

Startled, Meg looked into Mrs. Stein's eyes. Tiny wrinkles creased their edges, but this was no mocking smile on her face, no joke. She meant it. Meg thought she must be dreaming.

Mr. Stein stroked his chin, studying Meg. "What is your name, Miss?" His deep voice had an accent as thick as his wife's.

"Meg," she whispered. "Meg Kelly." She forced the words out a little louder.

Mr. Stein smiled. "We have three little boys, Meg." He patted the blond heads of his three sons. "My wife needs a daughter to help with so many men. Would you like to come with us to be our daughter? To help with the boys and the housework?"

"I'm with her." Mole clung to her arm. "She can't go without me, right Meg?"

Meg still couldn't find any words.

"We have three small boys already," Mr. Stein repeated, shaking his head slowly.

"Please, Mister," Mole said. "Please! I'll work real hard. I can be a farmer. I'm a real good farmer."

Mr. Stein laughed, a great booming sound in that small church. "You are too little to work so hard. What do you know of farming from New York City? There is no land there, only buildings."

Mrs. Stein answered him in German, but he shook his head and seemed to be arguing with her.

Meg held her breath, clenching her fists so tightly that her nails bit into the flesh of her palms. Then she let out her breath. It was no good caring. She forced herself to open her hands and stretch out her fingers.

But she couldn't fool herself. She did care. Desperately. A home, with lacy curtains at the window like she had seen on Main Street. She wanted it more than she had ever wanted anything. Under the folds of the brown shawl in her lap, Meg did something she hadn't done in years. She crossed her fingers, for luck.

When she looked up, Mr. Stein was nodding. "We will be a very big family. What is the brother's name?"

"Mole," he said.

"Mole?" Mrs. Stein raised an eyebrow. "What kind of a name is that for a boy? A grubby animal that burrows in the ground?"

"He was always so little, we just called him that." Meg finally found her voice. "His real name is Michael." Da had called him Michael before he was born, she remembered. It sounded strange to her now. No one else had ever used it.

Beside her, Mole smiled. "Michael," he whispered.

"Michael," Mrs. Stein said. "That is a name I like. Let us go, Meg and Michael, to settle with the agents."

With Meg's consent, Anna and Hugo Stein signed the papers releasing Meg and Mole into their care.

Mr. Wills stuck out his hand. "Let me be the first to wish you well."

"Remember," Miss Firth said, handing them a copy of the agreement, "you've guaranteed that the children will get schooling. One of our agents will keep in touch with you to make sure everything is working out satisfactorily."

Sean and Buffalo came over to bid farewell. They had found

places too. Both would be working for farmers. Only Birdie would be traveling on. The little girl sniffled once and rubbed her fist into her eye, but she turned away from Meg and walked off without a backward glance.

Meg didn't have time to think about her. With Mole clinging to her skirt, she followed the Steins out to their wagon in the schoolyard.

Mole had been quiet all the time inside, but he started coughing as soon as he got out in the cold night air.

"Oh no." Meg groaned. "Don't be sick now. They could still send us back." She spoke in a low voice, so only he could hear.

Anna told Meg to sit in the back and share the blanket with the middle boy, Johnny, who looked to be about five years old. Anna sat up next to Hugo and held the youngest boy, Robert, on her lap. Mole curled up close to Meg, and she wrapped the blanket Anna gave her around them both, even covering Mole's head, to muffle the sound of his coughing.

Freddie, the Stein's oldest boy, sat beside Mole with his own blanket. Freddie's white blond hair and pale blue eyes made him look younger than Mole, but he was at least six inches taller. He grinned at Meg when he saw her studying him and crossed his eyes, pulling a comical face.

Meg ignored him and tucked the blanket under her chin. The little boys, including Mole, fell asleep soon, but Meg stayed awake as the wagon climbed a steep road to the top of the bluffs and then went on and on over the dark, empty, rolling hills. Without a moon, she couldn't even see a road. Prairie stretched out forever in all directions.

After they had been traveling for an hour, the road dipped steeply down into a ravine. Meg blinked. Dark trees with ghostlike arms that stretched over the road. It was like going down into a dark hole or being swallowed up by the gaping earth. Meg shivered at the thought.

Finally, the wagon stopped at a stone farmhouse nestled under a hillside. Freddie led the way inside. Carrying Mole, Meg stumbled behind him, while Mr. and Mrs. Stein carried the other boys.

Mole never woke up as she lay him down beside Anna's boys on the big bed upstairs, where the roof slanted to meet the wall only a foot above the floor. She covered him with the thick quilt Mrs. Stein gave her. Then she followed Mrs. Stein to the other side of the room, separated by a curtain, to a smaller bed, neatly made.

"You have no nightgown?" Mrs. Stein asked as she turned back the covers.

Meg shook her head. She took off her shoes and tumbled into the bed with her clothes on. She was asleep even before Mrs. Stein blew out the candle.

CHAPTER 10: ANOTHER KIND OF TROUBLE

Meg woke before dawn and reached for Mole. He wasn't beside her. Where was he? She sat up. Then she remembered he was on the big bed on the other side of the loft. She had thought he was calling her. A dream, she decided. But then she heard him again, calling and moaning.

She jumped out of bed and raced over to him, her bare feet cold on the floorboards. Mrs. Stein was there before her. Meg hung back, unsure of what to do.

"Sh..." Mrs. Stein said. She covered him back up and lay a hand on his forehead.

"Meg," Mole cried and coughed, throwing the cover off again.

Meg squeezed past Mrs. Stein. "I'm here." She took up his hand. "So quit your blathering."

Mole didn't seem to hear her.

Mrs. Stein's lips pressed together in a hard line of disapproval. "Your brother is very sick. He is burning up with fever. You should have called a doctor."

"Where would I be finding a doctor?" Meg said angrily. "I can take care of him. I always have."

Mrs. Stein frowned, but otherwise ignored Meg's outburst. "How long has he been sick?" She dipped a rag in the washbasin beside the bed and lay it over Mole's forehead.

Meg shrugged. "A long time, I guess. I don't know how long.

Maybe since we started sleeping in the streets." She tucked the quilt back around Mole. "You're going to send us back now, ain't you?" she said without looking up.

"Ach no! Whatever gave you that idea?" Mrs. Stein tisked in disapproval. "But he needs a doctor now, and not just a sister."

Meg stood up to face her. "Is he going to die?"

Mrs. Stein patted Meg's shoulder. "Only God can answer that. We must pray for him."

Meg sniffed. She didn't know much about praying.

"You sit with him now," Mrs. Stein said. "Keep him covered."

Meg pulled the chair close enough to the bed to hold Mole's limp hand, willing him to open his eyes and look at her, but it was no good.

In a few minutes, Mrs. Stein returned with more rags and a fresh basin of cool water. She showed Meg how to wring out the rag in the water and smooth it down on Mole's forehead. "Keep him quiet while I get breakfast for my boys. I'll brew some willow tea for Michael too. That will help with the fever. Mr. Stein will go to town to fetch the doctor."

As soon as Mrs. Stein had gone downstairs, Meg stood up from beside Mole and took two quick steps across the room to the window. Even up here in the attic, there were lace curtains. She pushed them aside to look out. The yard between the house and the barn was bare, but beyond the barn the hill rose steeply, a maze with trees of yellow, orange and red.

Meg never thought she'd be looking through lace curtains at such beauty. Yet she would give it all up in an instant to have Mole well again.

What had she done, bringing the two of them way out here? Foolish for sure, to make Mole travel when he was so sick. She had meant no harm.. All she wanted was a home for herself and for Mole. She hadn't thought about Mole getting sick. Ma had always said she was selfish, and now she knew it was true.

Before she had time for any more dismal thoughts, Mrs. Stein came in with a bowl of porridge and a cup of willow tea for Mole. "Are you hungry?" she asked Meg.

Meg shook her head. She had forgotten about being hungry.

"Well, take yourself down to the kitchen anyway, and eat now." Mrs. Stein bent over her workbasket and handed Meg a pair of woolen socks. "You'll need these. After you've eaten, I want you to take my boys outside. They'll show you around. I'll sit with your brother and feed him if he wakes up."

"I better stay with him." Meg took the socks, but didn't move. "He calls for me sometimes."

Mrs. Stein shook her head. "I'll be right here with him all the time. You'll make yourself sick too if you don't eat right."

Meg pressed her lips together stubbornly. She didn't have to listen to this small, soft woman. She couldn't make her do anything.

Mole lay very still on the bed as Mrs. Stein replaced the cloth once more. He didn't even know she was there. Mrs. Stein didn't argue with Meg. She just went on as if Meg had already agreed.

Meg sagged, her defiance draining out of her like water in a sieve. There was no sense in arguing. She put on the new socks and the shoes from the Children's Aid Society, then went slowly down the steep, narrow steps to the kitchen.

Bright sunlight shone through the lace curtains hanging in the kitchen window, making the room look clean and fresh. Meg scooped up some porridge for herself from the pot that bubbled on a shiny cookstove in one corner of the kitchen.

The Stein boys sprawled on the wood floor in front of the hearth. They looked up from their game of marbles to stare at her, but Meg ignored them, her thoughts on Mole. She sat on the bench at the table with her back to them, eating quickly, even though the porridge was tasteless.

Gradually she was aware that the biggest boy, Freddie, had walked around the table to stand in front of her. He started talking as soon as she looked up. "Mama says you're our new sister." Freddie was a lot bigger than Mole, but she guessed he was younger. His face had a kind of roundness to it that Mole's had never had.

Johnny and Robert sidled around the table to join Freddie. They stood in a row, staring at her, all alike, with straw-blond hair, pale blue eyes, and soft, round faces. Robert stuck his thumb in his mouth.

Meg stood up, pushing the bench back. "Your ma said I should go out with you, for you to show me the place. Do you have jackets?"

"Course we do," Freddie said. The jackets hung on a row of pegs beside the front door. Freddie could just reach his. He shrugged it on, while Meg got Robert's and Johnny's. None of the jackets were new, but they looked warm, and there were no holes. Far better than anything she or Mole had ever had before coming west. Meg frowned at the sight of them all bundled up so neatly. Not a one of them had any idea how lucky they were. She put on her own brown shawl, and they went out.

Freddie ran ahead as soon as the door closed. Johnny raced after him, trying to catch up. Robert didn't even try. He plodded along with his thumb in his mouth, his eyes darting back and forth.

Meg took Robert's hand and tried to hurry him after Freddie. Freddie was running across an open field beside the house, but thick woods climbed the hills on three sides of the valley. Meg didn't want to lose sight of Freddie or the house.

The sky overhead was blue, empty of any clouds. Empty of anything at all, for that matter, and huge. Meg pulled on Robert's arm, hurrying him as much as she could without pulling him off his feet. If Freddie went into the woods, he could be gone before she blinked. Then she'd never find her way back.

Suddenly a huge black and white animal with horns lumbered in front of them.

"Watch out!" Meg screamed. She shoved Robert behind her.

Freddie turned to look where Meg was pointing. Then he laughed. "That's just Lotte, our cow. She wouldn't hurt anyone."

Meg scowled. "I know that," she lied. "I just didn't want Robert to run into it." She glared at him, daring him to laugh again.

Freddie sauntered up to the cow and patted her flank.

"You come walk beside me now," Meg said to him. "I don't want you running on ahead."

"What if I don't want to?" he taunted her. "You can't catch me."

She surprised him, darting forward and grabbing his arm before he had gone two steps. "Maybe I don't know cows, but I know running, and I know fighting. You mind me or else!" She dug her fingers into the roundness of his arm and shook him like a rag. She didn't have to put up with sass from this little brat half her size.

He squealed and tried to pull free.

Johnny pulled at her shawl, crying. "Don't hurt him."

Meg stared at her own whitened knuckles and realized what she was doing. She dropped his arm, her face burning. No smart-aleck little kid was worth trouble like this would bring.

Freddie fell backwards at his sudden release. He scrambled to his feet, rubbing his arm. He would probably tell on her, and then she and Mole would be kicked out. It was her stupid temper, making her do things she never meant to do.

She scowled. Now where were the other two?

Johnny was close by, looking anxiously from one to the other, but Robert had disappeared. Meg spun frantically looking for the little boy. She spotted him a hundred yards back, sitting down in the pasture. With one thumb in his mouth, he plucked at the dried grass.

"C'mon," Meg called crossly.

"His legs are too short for much walking." Freddie kept his distance, still rubbing his sore arm. "You'll have to carry him."

Meg walked back to the little boy and stood over him with her hands on her hips.

Robert didn't even look up.

Meg pulled him to his feet, but he sank down again. She scooped him up, set him on her hip and glared at Freddie. He had no business being right.

He stuck out his tongue at her, but didn't come any closer. He took a stick and began shooing Lotte toward the barn. Meg followed, stumbling over the uneven ground, littered with sticks and clumps of roots.

Robert snuggled into her, with his head resting on her shoulder. He grew heavier with each step.

Outside the house Meg put Robert down and shook her aching arms. "You can walk from here."

Just before going inside, Johnny slipped his hand into hers. "I'm scared of Lotte too," he whispered.

Meg shook free of him and pushed on inside. "Who said I was scared?" she demanded.

When Mr. Stein finally came with the doctor, Meg hovered by the door of the attic bedroom, feeling useless. The doctor poked and prodded Mole, listened to him breathe and felt his forehead. Mole tossed feverishly on the bed, unaware of the doctor.

The doctor gave Mrs. Stein a packet of powders with a paper of instructions for dosing him, and said he'd be back the next day to check on the boy. He smiled at Mrs. Stein and pinched Meg's cheek, telling her not to worry. "If we can get the fever to break, we should see great improvement by morning."

Mrs. Stein allowed Meg to stay with Mole while the family ate at noon, but she came upstairs right after eating and replaced the cool cloth Meg had just smoothed over Mole's forehead. "I've put the little ones down for their nap. I'll stay with your brother while you eat. Then you and Freddie wash up the dishes."

"I'm not very hungry," Meg said. "Can't I just stay with him?"

Mrs. Stein shook her head, frowning slightly. "You must be hungry. We must get some meat on your bones before winter sets in, or you'll get as sick as your brother." Mrs. Stein sat down heavily in the rocker and leaned her head back. "And I must rest. Mr. Stein is right. I mustn't work too hard."

Meg took Mole's hand in her own, but he didn't stir.

"Go eat before your dinner gets cold," Mrs. Stein said without opening her eyes. "Then wash the dishes."

As soon as she had finished eating, Meg took hot water from the cookstove and poured it in a basin with a little soft soap. "Come dry these," she ordered Freddie as she began washing.

"You can't boss me around," Freddie argued, but he gathered up his marbles into a leather pouch and shoved them into his pocket. He took a clean rag to dry the dishes, keeping the table between them.

The work reminded Meg of washing dishes in New York. When they lived in the back house, she had to take the three cracked plates outside for bucket of cold water to rinse them in. Usually, they just wiped them off and didn't bother with washing

But Meg remembered before that, when they had lived in a room with a window. Ma used to fill a basin full of hot, sudsy water.

She would tie a big flowered apron around Meg and then stand her up on a stool to help. Sometimes Ma even sang, songs like "Good Luck to the Barley Mow." Meg had no idea what it meant, but she remembered laughing as she echoed Ma's lines.

"Bet you can't read." Freddie's plopped down onto the bench beside the work table, interrupting her thoughts. "Papa says no one in New York goes to school."

"Your Papa's right about one thing. I've never been to school. But I can read." Meg shook her head clear away the past. It was no use remembering Ma. She was gone now, and that was the end of it.

"I go to school," Freddie said. "I'm the best reader in the first grade."

Meg swished the rag over the next plate.

"I didn't go today," Freddie continued, "on account of you and your brother coming. Papa says you'll likely be in the first grade with me."

Meg froze in mid-swish. She had forgotten that the orphans sent west were promised schooling. Da had set a great store by that. A person who went to school would never be trapped in a factory where the dye turned your hands blue like Ma's.

"But you're just an orphan," Freddie chattered on. "That means you got nobody."

"I got a brother." Meg kept her tone neutral.

"We ain't keeping him," Freddie teased. "We don't need another boy around here. I heard Papa say so." Freddie edged away and looked at her slyly. "Besides, he's awful sick. Probably he'll die. Mama's last baby died."

Meg spun around, dropping the tin plate she was scrubbing. She grabbed Freddie's arm. "Don't you ever say that!" She slapped him.

"Mama!" Freddie screamed.

Meg let go of his arm and stepped back, horrified by what she had done. The tin plate she had dropped rattled around and around until it finally came to rest by her foot. Freddie whimpered, his cheek red where her hand hit.

Mrs. Stein rushed downstairs. "It's all right." She folded Freddie into her big arms and pulled him close to hug him.

Meg trembled. She didn't care if they sent her away, she lied to herself. There was nothing so special about this place. She scowled down at the floor and wrapped her arms around herself.

Mrs. Stein sent Freddie out to chop kindling and sighed. "He can be such a tease," she said, but her lips were set in the same hard, thin line of disapproval that she'd had earlier. "It's all right. I'll finish the dishes if you sit with your brother."

"No." Meg's voice was a whispered croak. She cleared her throat. "No," she said again, more clearly. "You sit a little longer. I'll finish up."

Mrs. Stein smiled a tired half-smile and patted her hand. "That's a good girl, Meg."

Meg finished the dishes by herself. No one had called her a good girl since Da died. Ma never thought she was any good. What did Mrs. Stein know about her? Meg swished the cloth on the porridge pot and scrubbed. When Mrs. Stein found out what Ma had always known, she wouldn't want Meg around anymore, but it didn't matter. Just as soon as Mole got better, she could take care of herself and Mole too.

They didn't need anyone else!

CHAPTER 11: MA WAS RIGHT ALL ALONG

Mole stirred without really waking up late that afternoon. Hot and restless, he threw off the covers, but in minutes he was shivering again. He cried out frantically, but Meg couldn't tell what he said. His cries set him coughing so hard he could barely breathe.

Mrs. Stein came to check on them as the shadows lengthened. "Run downstairs, Meg, and bring the flax seed tea I brewed," Mrs. Stein told her as she tucked the little boy in again and replaced the wet cloth on his forehead.

"I think he's calling for me," Meg said.

Mrs. Stein frowned. "He's delirious. He needs the tea more than he needs you sitting there. Go on."

The words stung. Didn't Mole need her? Shaken, Meg obeyed.

By the time she returned, Mole was quiet again. Mrs. Stein stirred honey into the tea and fed it to him by spoonfuls, along with the powders the doctor had left. Meg held his hand, watching helplessly while Mrs. Stein did all the things she didn't know how to do.

The day dragged on. Meg fretted, hating to leave Mole's side and frustrated at the chores Mrs. Stein set her. The work wasn't hard, not nearly as tiring as selling apples, but she wasn't used to being told what to do and the orders, however kindly given, galled.

At supper time, Mole was still tossing restlessly, so Mrs. Stein sent Meg to peel potatoes.

Mr. Stein came in while Meg bent over the fire, stirring the stew his wife had made in a big iron kettle that morning. Meg had peeled a dozen potatoes, added them to the pot, and then thickened it with a handful of cornmeal according to the older woman's instructions.

Holding his hands out to the fire to warm them, Mr. Stein turned his head toward Meg. "The little boy is still sick?" His voice was deep and quiet.

Meg nodded.

Mr. Stein's dark eyebrows drew together in a frown. "And my wife is working just as hard as ever."

Meg didn't answer. She hadn't meant to bring them trouble. She was trying to help.

Mrs. Stein insisted Meg eat supper, then asked her to wash the dishes, wipe the board table clean and sweep the kitchen. Finally, Mrs. Stein let her carry a candle upstairs to sit with Mole, while she went downstairs to brew some more flaxseed tea and fix up a bed for her boys in front of the hearth.

Meg sat on the edge of the bed and squeezed Mole's hand. "Don't you go dying on me too, Mole," she whispered fiercely.

Mole lay buried up to his chin in quilts. The bright red flush on his cheeks emphasized his pallor. A couple of times he called out for Meg, but he never opened his eyes.

"I'm right here," she told him, squeezing his hand as if that could undo the knot in her stomach. "Don't be worrying."

He never seemed to hear.

As the candle burned lower, Meg heard Mrs. Stein settling the boys on the makeshift bed beside the hearth. Short bursts of laughter drifted upstairs, followed by the low murmur of Mrs. Stein telling the little ones a bedtime story. Gradually the house quieted so the creak of the rocker on the floor boards could be heard.

After a bit, Mr. Stein told his wife she ought to go to bed. Meg felt her own eyes getting gritty, and she longed to sleep, but she shook her head to clear it.

Mr. Stein's heavy footsteps coming into the room startled her out of a light doze. "You should go to bed now, too," he suggested. "I'll stay with your brother."

"I can't be leaving him now." She twisted the end of her shawl round and round her thumb. "I won't fall asleep."

Mr. Stein didn't answer for a minute. "You have a family now," he said finally. "That means we all help each other."

Meg didn't answer. She knew Mr. Stein was trying to be kind, but words were easy. As far as she could tell, having a family hadn't meant anything. She and Mole couldn't count on anyone else, but they had each other. He was her brother. She'd stay with him.

Mr. Stein watched her for a moment, then he nodded slowly and thumped back downstairs.

The moon rose, filling the attic room with a soft glow that fell across Mole's face, hiding the gaunt shadows left by weeks of hunger. Then moonlight slid on past the window, slipping away like a dream, leaving the room in soft darkness.

Meg jumped up, alarmed at her brother's pallor. She leaned over him. His breathing was shallow and ragged, but it hadn't stopped. She eased back into the chair. Slowly her eyes drifted shut.

Some hours later, Meg awoke with a jerk from a clattering at the foot of the stairs. She heard Mr. Stein fumbling with the lantern. Meg leapt to her feet and saw that Mole was no longer in the bed. With her heart pounding, she tumbled down the stairs, almost falling on top of the small body crumpled on the bottom step.

"Meg," she heard his raspy whisper as Mr. Stein scooped him up off the floor.

Meg reached toward him, but Mrs. Stein took her arm and pulled her away. "He's sleepwalking," she said in a hushed voice. "You don't want to wake him up."

Meg tried to shake free of her grasp. "He's never done that before. Let me go to him."

Mrs. Stein did not let go. "It's the fever. He doesn't know you." Meg would have argued, but she could see the vacant stare in Mole's eyes. They were open, but it was clear he didn't see her or anyone else. She followed as Mr. Stein carried her brother up the stairs.

Mr. Stein laid Mole back in the bed. Mrs. Stein pushed Meg aside to cover the little boy with the quilt. Then she smoothed a fresh cool cloth on his forehead.

He tossed his head back and forth as if searching for her in vain. He clutched the quilt and called for Meg over and over before lapsing back into a deeper sleep. Meg wormed in past both Mr. and Mrs. Stein to take Mole's small, hot hand. She stroked it with her own.

Mrs. Stein touched her shoulder. "You go to sleep now. I'll sit with him."

"I can do it," Meg protested. She hadn't meant to fall asleep earlier.

"No," Mrs. Stein insisted. "You'll make yourself sick too. That wouldn't help your brother any. Go on. You're not alone anymore. You don't have to take care of everything."

Meg narrowed her eyes. Why did Mrs. Stein always have to tell her what to do? She hadn't needed anyone to do that for a long time.

But this was the Stein's house. What choice did she have but to obey them? Still frowning, she went back to the room she had slept in the night before and lay down, determined to stay awake and listen for Mole. She kept her eyes wide open, staring at the ceiling. Both of the Steins had insisted she wasn't alone anymore. What did they know? Meg thought she had never felt quite so alone in all her life.

In spite of her determination to stay awake, Meg fell asleep again. When she woke, it was light. She shook off the quilt and ran into Mole's room.

Mole lay absolutely still on the big bed.

For one horrible minute, Meg thought he was dead. Her hands flew to her mouth, as if by force of will she could stop the truth from coming out. She wanted to run, just like she had run from Ma, but her feet wouldn't move.

Meg closed her eyes, forcing all thoughts of Ma away. This was Mole. She couldn't leave him. She clenched her fists, then opened them slowly. Step by step, she made her way to the bedside and took hold of his hand.

It was cool, but not cold. As she leaned over him, Meg could tell his breathing was easier too. She felt shaky with relief.

Mrs. Stein slipped into the room and smiled. "He is better this morning." She lowered herself into the rocker and picked up her work basket. "You go eat now. I left porridge on the stove."

Meg hesitated. "You'll call me if he wakes up?"

"Sure, sure. Don't worry." Mrs. Stein selected a worn sock. She put a polished wooden darning egg inside, then threaded her needle.

Meg ate quickly and washed up the dishes while Johnny watched her silently and Robert played on the floor with a carved wooden horse. Freddie was gone, probably to school. Meg was wiping the table when the doctor came in. Meg hung the dish towel on the rack by the oven and followed the doctor upstairs.

The doctor set his black leather bag on the floor beside the bed. "Now then, what have we here?" He leaned over Mole, lay a hand on his forehead, and then felt the back of his neck. "Hmm," the doctor muttered. He opened his bag and took out a wooden tube that flared into a wide bell at one end.

Meg, hovering by the doorway, saw Mole's eyes widen.

The doctor lifted Mole's shirt and placed the bell end of the tube to the little's boy's chest. The doctor inserted the narrow end of the tube in one ear and listened intently. "Deep breath, my boy," he instructed.

Meg realized she had been holding her own breath and let it go in a rush.

The doctor helped Mole sit up and listened in the same way to his back. He thumped a knuckle along Mole's spine before helping him lie down again.

"Malnutrition," he pronounced. "No doubt about that. But we can be thankful the worst of the fever is over." He packed away his tools. "Keep him quiet for a few days more, and I think he'll be just fine. I'm sure you'll be able to fatten him up once we get him on his feet."

Meg felt the blood rush to her cheeks. He would be all right. Never mind she hadn't been able to find enough food for them both. Never mind she had let him get sick. None of that mattered if he just got better.

Mrs. Stein went downstairs with the doctor, finally leaving Meg alone with Mole. His eyes were open and looked like two black spots in a platter of milk.

"You ain't mad at me, Meg, are you?" he asked with a tremor in his voice. "You ain't going off and leaving me now, are you? You ain't sending me back?"

"Oh, hush up." She brushed the hair off his forehead. "I told you and told you I wasn't, didn't I? You just keep on getting better. Stop fretting or you'll make yourself worse."

"But you did leave me," Mole said. "I woke up, and I couldn't see you anywhere. She told me you wasn't gone, but I didn't believe her."

"I wasn't gone," Meg said, "just downstairs." She had tried to stay with him. It wasn't her fault Mrs. Stein wouldn't let her, was it? "Just hush up, and try to get better." She settled into the chair beside the bed and held his hand until he fell asleep again.

Two days later, Mole was allowed to get up for supper. Mr. Stein carried him down the stairs and set him at the trestle table. For a minute, Freddie, Robert, and Johnny just stared at Mole. Mole stared back at them, looking small and alone on the bench.

Then Freddie stepped forward. "Want to see my marbles?" he said. "I've got a real agate."

"You can show him after supper," Mrs. Stein said. "Meg, help them all wash up now. It's time to eat."

Mr. Stein took a long time with the grace that night, thanking the Lord for letting Michael and Meg join their family and for Michael's recovery. Meg was sure glad for Mole's recovery, but she wasn't so sure what the Steins had to be thankful for. It seemed to her she and Mole had only brought them trouble.

Mole's eyes kept straying to the steaming roast and the big bowl of boiled potatoes on the table in front of Mr. Stein. Meg poked her elbow into his ribs to remind him to keep his head bowed. He squirmed away from her elbow and didn't take his eyes off the food.

Finally, Mr. Stein finished the prayer. He began cutting the roast and dishing it out onto each tin plate.

"Did you ever see so much food, Meg?" Mole whispered.

Mrs. Stein overheard him, and patted his head. "You won't be hungry here, Michael. Eat up. It will do you good."

Meg scowled. He hadn't exactly been starving before, thanks to her. She had looked after him. She hadn't meant to let him get sick. No one could blame her for not trying.

"Tomorrow is Saturday." Mr. Stein passed a full plate to Meg. "On Monday, you must go with Freddie to school." Startled, Meg looked up at Mr. Stein and just as quickly, looked down again. It wouldn't do any good to get her hopes up.

Mr. Stein sliced more roast and piled it on the plate for Mole, who took it eagerly, as if still afraid it might be snatched from him.

"What about me?" Mole piped up as Mr. Stein dished Johnny's plate full. "I'm old enough to go to school."

"Ja." Mr. Stein paused with the carving knife in the air to look into Mole's eyes. "But you are too small still. It is two miles to walk and you have been very sick. We'll keep you here for now and fatten you up a bit. When spring comes, then you can go to school with the others."

"But I want to go with them now."

"Be patient, Michael," Mr. Stein said. "You'll go to school yet."

Meg kicked Mole under the table. He ought to be happy just to have a roof over his head. "You never wanted to learn to read in New York. How come you're so set on school now?"

"I just want to," Mole said stubbornly. He pouted through the rest of the meal.

Meg paid him no mind. School. Just thinking of it made her heart thump. Da had talked of schooling. Maybe coming here had been a good choice after all.

The next morning, Mole came down for breakfast looking brighter than he ever had. Mrs. Stein called him over to her after they ate. "How old are you, Michael?"

He shrugged and looked to Meg.

"He's six," Meg said.

"My Freddie, he is six also. I think his boots from last winter will fit you. They are still too big for Johnny."

Mole tried on the old boots and let Mrs. Stein do up the laces for him. "Golly, these really fit," he said. He danced across the kitchen, and around the table. "Lookee here, Meg! I got brand new boots and they really fit. Real boots, Meg."

"If you're feeling good enough to do that much scampering, you might just as well go on outside, now you got boots," Meg said sourly. Hadn't she tried to get boots for him?

"Run along outside, all of you." Mrs. Stein shooed the boys out.

"But stay in the yard."

They ran out, with the door banging shut behind them. Mrs. Stein chuckled, then turned to Meg. "Do you know how to sew?"

"A little," Meg said. "Ma . . . she used to sew when I was little. She taught me some before Da died." She bit her lip. She hadn't meant to say so much.

"Ach, ja. I remember New York. A terrible place to be alone. I don't know how I could have managed without Mr. Stein. I can just imagine how hard it was for your mama to raise a family without your papa," Mrs. Stein said sympathetically.

Meg pressed her lips together in a thin line. "We managed, Mrs. Stein." She didn't want to talk about them. A burning ache in her gut filled her and threatened to spill out in tears. She ducked her head and blinked her eyes rapidly, forcing the tears back. She never cried. Ma had always said it was no use boiling your cabbage twice. Ma and Da had died, and it was no use crying about it. She'd shed no tears, especially not in front of Mrs. Stein. How could she understand anything about Meg?

Mrs. Stein laid a hand on Meg's shoulder. "We are a new family now. You must call me Anna, and Mr. Stein is Hugo." She didn't wait for Meg to agree. She showed Meg a wicker basket full of clothes. "I have mending. My boys, they go through the elbows and knees as fast as I can fix them." She lowered herself into the rocker and smiled. "Shall we work on these together?"

Meg sat on the floor beside her. Anna. She mouthed the words to get the feel of them. Anna and Hugo. They were comfortable names, easier than Mr. and Mrs. Stein. Could they really become a family?

Anna and Meg worked without talking. Meg was grateful for the silence. At least here was something she knew how to do. She had mended Mole's and her own clothes so many times there was little left but patches. Some of the anger seeped out of her in the quiet calm of the kitchen, when the only sounds were the flickering of the fire on the hearth, the softly bubbling stew in the kettle and the creaking of Anna's rocking chair. This work beat selling apples on a rainy street corner.

They sewed in silence for nearly an hour. Suddenly Johnny burst in the door. "Mama," he screamed. "Freddie and Michael are fighting something awful! Down by the barn. I think they're killing each other!"

Meg leapt up and ran out the door. Her first thought was to save Mole. He was much smaller. He'd just been sick. Freddie must have started it, bullying Mole.

She reached the barn before anyone else. The two boys rolled in the dirt and scraps of old straw. Robert had backed up against a stall, and covered his eyes with his hands. Mole sat on top, jabbing his fists into Freddie's while Freddie warded off the blows as best he could.

Both boys were crying as they punched each other. Blood ran from Mole's nose, but he wouldn't stop. For an instant, Meg felt a fierce pride. Mole could take care of himself. Even sick, even half starved, he could take care of himself. She had taught him that.

Then she realized what the Steins would think of it. Young city hooligans, always fighting. Suddenly angry, Meg grabbed Mole's collar and jerked him off Freddie.

"You little fool!" she screamed at him, shaking him by the shoulders. "What do you think you're doing? You want to get sent back to New York?"

"But, Meg," he cried, struggling to pull loose from her. "He said we was orphan rats." Tears streamed down his cheeks, mixing with the blood from his nose and the dirt from the floor. "Don't be mad at me. I couldn't help it. I had to fight him."

"I don't care what he said." Meg shook him with each clipped word, forgetting how mad she had been at Freddie such a short time ago.

"Don't you care none about me?" Mole stopped pulling against her. Bits of straw stuck in his hair.

Freddie scrambled to his feet. His shirt was torn at the collar, and his face was streaked with tears.

Anna lumbered into the barn. She was panting from hurrying so much. She pulled Mole away from Meg and gathered both boys to her in a big hug. Clucking softly, she used her apron to wipe the blood and grime from each tear-streaked face.

Mole peeked around Anna's skirt to Meg as she stood near the barn door, her fists clenched tight and her jaw set. "Please?" His lips formed the word silently.

Meg glared at him. Please what? She didn't know what he was asking. She wrenched her eyes away from his grimy face to stare at the dust dancing in the cold sunlight pouring in through the barn door.

From the corner of her eye she saw him look away from her. She watched while he let Anna lead him and Freddie back up to the house. Meg didn't move.

Johnny slipped up beside her and took her hand, but she shook him off. He took Robert's hand instead and followed the others, leaving Meg alone.

Meg stood for a long time in the barn, clenching her fists until the nails broke the skin on her palms. She didn't know she could get so angry at Mole, angry enough to hit him. She saw again his pleading eyes, and she choked back a shuddering sob. She wanted to cuddle him, make him a baby again, make him need her again. She would never have stayed mad at him. Anna had come too soon. Anna had taken him away from her.

The barn door creaked in the wind. Meg shivered. It was cold outside. There was no point staying here anymore. Wearily, Meg went back up to the house.

Mole and Freddie sat at the table, sharing an apple. Johnny and Robert munched on another one. Mrs. Stein didn't look up. Meg picked up her mending and started in where she had left off. She sewed on the patches, concentrating only on her needle and the stitches. But the peaceful calm of earlier was gone.

At noon, Hugo came in from the field for dinner. He listened to Anna's account of the fight. Shaking his head, he stood both boys in front of him and frowned. "Friedrich, Michael." He looked at each one in turn. "You are brothers now; we're a family now. Families don't fight each other. Families help each other."

Once, Meg thought, Da might have said the same. But he had left his family; left them to fend for themselves. What kind of family had they been?

By the time they finished the noon meal, Mole and Freddie had forgotten their fight. Mole helped Freddie with his chores of filling the wood box and bringing in water, then they left the little boys in the house and went out to catch rabbits in the field.

"Shouldn't he rest?" Meg worried.

"No, no. Running will make him stronger. Don't worry. It's good for youngsters to be outside on such a fine day," Anna handed her the broom. "Finish sweeping up. I'll pour the cream into the churn for you."

Meg was wrestling with the butter churn when Mole burst through the door. In his hand he carried a large, fuzzy, orange and black caterpillar.

"Look, Meg, look! They got bugs here I never ever seen before, and Freddie says there'll be millions more come spring."

Meg pulled back from the caterpillar in his outstretched hand. "Take it outside. Can't you ever leave off about bugs?"

"It's all right," Anna interrupted. "It's just a woolly bear. It won't hurt anything."

Mole slipped past Meg and brought the caterpillar to show Anna. Meg slammed the dasher down in the churn with all her strength.

On Sunday morning the kitchen was filled with activity as they hurried to get ready for church. The only dress Meg had was the one she wore every day. She shook the wrinkles out of it before putting it on. Anna had an extra shirt of Freddie's that Mole could wear. Meg spit on her fingers and smoothed down his hair. His face, fresh and clean, was shining with excitement. He had never looked so good before.

"Come here, Michael," Anna said, coming into the kitchen from her bedroom. "Let me comb your hair."

Mole skipped over to her, leaving Meg alone at the table.

Hugo had hitched the team to the wagon by the time Anna had all the boys ready to go.

Meg recognized the church as soon as they drove up to it as they place they had first come to town. Reverend Aleer greeted her and Mole like old friends, but Meg hung back from his enthusiasm. She shook his hand awkwardly when he offered it and mumbled her own greeting in return.

During the service, Meg tried to do as Anna did, standing and sitting according to her lead. When it was time to sing, she listened without opening her mouth. Anna frowned at her, and pointed to the words in the hymnal, but Meg didn't know how to sing. She shrugged.

Mole, stuck between her and Hugo, didn't squirm any more than Freddie, on the other side of Hugo. She poked him once or twice when it looked like he wasn't paying much attention, but she had a hard time following the minister herself.

Meg sighed in relief when the service ended and the adults gathered in the churchyard to exchange greetings while the children darted in and out among them playing tag. Anna introduced Meg to their closest neighbor, Ruth Hermann, a tall woman with a sharp nose.

Ruth's daughter, Sally, took Meg's arm. "Come sit with me on the wagon." Sally was nearly as tall as her mother, but fair-haired. A couple of pale ringlets hung loose from a broad-brimmed bonnet and framed her pretty face. She pulled Meg along behind her to the wagons. "I want to hear all about New York. Mama saw it when she came over on the ship with her mama. She says it's no place for a young girl, but I bet it's exciting."

Mole had been playing tag with Freddie, but now he ran up to her and grabbed her hand. "Where are you going?" he demanded.

Meg shook her hand free. "I'm not going anywhere. Can't you just let me sit down?"

Freddie darted past, punching Mole on the shoulder. "You're it," he shouted. "Bet you can't catch me."

Mole hesitated, looking first at Meg, then at Freddie and back to Meg.

Meg gave him a little shove. "Go on and play. I'm not going anywhere." As if to demonstrate she sat down beside Sally on wagon tongue. The horses, unhitched before the service, stood head to tail a little ways off in the shade of the tree.

Mole gave in and darted after Freddie, but not without looking back once more.

"Little brothers can be such pests," Sally declared, smoothing out the pinafore covering her dress. "I don't know how you can stand it with four of them."

They were still talking, or at least Sally was talking and Meg was still listening, when Freddie and Mole came back ten minutes later to sit in the shade under the wagon. The two of them were so quiet, Meg grew suspicious. She leaned over to look down at them and saw they were sharing licks on a long stick of candy.

"Where did you get that?" she asked.

Freddie squirmed uncomfortably. "It was Michael's."

"Where did you get it?" she asked Mole.

Mole edged further away from her. "It was just kind of sitting

106

there. I figured no one wanted it."

Meg bent down, grabbed his collar, and dragged him out. "So you stole it." She shook him, rattling his teeth. "I thought you didn't want to get sent back. What makes you think anybody will want to stay with a thief?"

Freddie scrambled out from under the wagon and pulled on her arm. "Leave go!" he yelled.

Mole started crying.

Sally touched Meg's shoulder and said, "I think you're hurting him."

Meg let go of Mole so suddenly that he fell to the ground. He scrabbled away from her and stood up, slapping at the dust on his pants. Meg looked down at her hands. She had been shaking him just like Jake had done. What had happened to her? How could she be so angry all the time? She turned abruptly and strode away from the wagon.

Mole caught up to her on the other side of the church. "Meg? Where are you going?"

"You can't be stealing things, not anything," she said, without looking at him. "You're going to get sent back."

"You keep going on and on about that." He sniffled and wiped his nose on his sleeve. "But you stole Jake's watch."

Startled, Meg raised her hand, as if to ward off that horrible truth.

But obviously Mole took it wrong. "Don't hit me, Meg." He took several steps back. "I know it. I saw you playing with it. If you get sent back for that, I want to go too."

Meg let her hand drop to her side. She felt as if he had kicked her in the stomach. She couldn't say anything.

"I won't tell anyone." Mole inched a bit forward. "I know that Danny stole it from you." When she still said nothing, he took another step toward her. "I ain't mad about my cap anymore. It's okay. Really." He reached out and tentatively patted her hand. "Everybody does it."

Freddie caught up to them, but hung back a few feet. He darted his eyes from one to the other. Then he cocked his head sideways. "Hey, Michael, there's some other kids from school here. Let's go play crack the whip with them."

Mole hesitated. "Meg?" He touched her hand once more, but

when Meg still didn't answer, he let Freddie pull him away.

Meg watched Mole run off through the crowd. Ma had been right all along. Meg hadn't done much good at all taking care of him, not if she couldn't even teach him stealing was wrong. He needed a real Mama, someone like Anna, not a selfish fool like herself. She had thought all she needed was to find a family.

Well, it was obvious Mole needed a family, someone to teach him right from wrong.

But it was too late for her.

CHAPTER 12: TOO SELFISH FOR FAMILY

On Monday morning, Freddie ran upstairs, shouting. "Meg, Mama says hurry up or you'll be late for school."

Meg's stomach lurched. She had forgotten about school. "I'm coming," she called and hurried downstairs.

Mole was waiting. His eyes were round and moist, like he was trying hard not to cry. Anna handed Meg a wooden bowl of cornmeal mush from the iron pot bubbling on the cook stove.

Meg poured a little maple syrup on it and took a bite. She really wasn't very hungry.

Mole squeezed up beside her and leaned against her arm.

"Shove over." She elbowed him. "Where's your breakfast?"

"I don't want any." He shook his head so hard that his hair fell into his eyes.

Meg smoothed it back with her fingers. "Go on. You have to eat something."

Mole grabbed her hand. "You're coming back, ain't you? Can you promise me you'll come back?"

Meg freed her hand from his grip. "Stop your blathering. Of course I'm coming back."

Freddie grabbed his jacket and pulled open the front door. "Hurry up, Meg. It's time to go."

Meg still held her half full bowl of mush. She shoved it at Mole.

"Here, eat this. It will be good for you." She grabbed her shawl and headed out the door.

Mole grabbed her skirt. "Meg?"

She pulled her skirt free of him. This was her first chance ever to go to school. He shouldn't spoil it for her. "I'm coming back," she said impatiently and pushed out the door.

At the edge of the clearing she looked back. Mole stood beside the front door, looking very tiny against the stone walls. She waved, but he didn't wave back. Meg kicked a stone down the path. When she looked up, Mole hadn't moved. She kicked the stone again.

Freddie skipped ahead most of the way. Meg didn't mind. The path was easy to follow. Yellow birches and red maples lined the edges. Piles of leaves crunched underfoot. Meg breathed deeply of the cool, crisp air, and firmly locked away thoughts of Mole standing alone in the doorway.

As they neared the schoolhouse, Freddie let her catch up to him. He took her hand and pulled her toward the fresh pine-board cabin. "I'll introduce you to Miss Thomson. All the others mostly know who you are, because I told them all about you."

The school yard was a flat, bare, dirt space, packed hard by scores of feet playing tag and jump rope. Two dozen boys and girls crowded around her. A couple of them looked younger than Mole and a few more seemed older than she was. Most of them were somewhere in between. Freddie told her all their names, but Meg didn't listen.

"What's it like to ride on a train?" one boy asked.

"Tell me about New York," a girl said. "Are the buildings there really higher than any trees?"

Meg didn't answer any of them. She was relieved when Sally came into the school yard.

Sally put her arm around Meg. "Hello, neighbor." Sally beamed. "We can be special friends at school 'cuz we know each other. C'mon. I'll show you where everything is."

Meg let herself be escorted around the school yard, even though there wasn't much to see. Sally pointed out the two outhouses near the trees, and a swing hanging from the big elm shading the schoolyard. "The swing's nice," Sally said. "But most times the boys get there first."

Soon a slim, young woman came out on the school steps and

rang a hand bell. The children lined up, boys on one side and girls on the other. At the teacher's signal, they filed inside. In the middle of the room, near the front, a black, potbellied stove took up the space of several desks. No fire was lit in it right now, and the room was a little chilly, but not uncomfortable. The teacher's desk stood at the front of the room, and the children's desks lined up in straight rows with an aisle down the center facing hers.

The teacher shook Meg's hand and led her to the front of the room. "I'm Miss Thomson. And you must be Meg Kelly. Freddie's told us so much about you." She turned Meg to face the class.

"Class, say good morning to Meg Kelly, from New York," Miss Thomson said. "I'm sure she has a great many stories to share with us."

The children scraped their chairs and benches back to stand up. "Good morning, Meg Kelly," they recited in unison.

Meg barely heard them. She was looking at the shelf of books beside Miss Thomson's desk. There must have been a dozen or more books on it . The wall behind the desk was covered by a large blackboard and a colored map, but Meg's eyes kept coming back to the books. She had never seen so many in one place.

Miss Thomson spent a few minutes questioning Meg about her previous schooling, then showed Meg to a desk for her to share with another student. The girl was much younger, Freddie's age, and Meg realized Miss Thomson had placed her in the same grade as Freddie. "I can read," she told Miss Thomson again.

"I know that." Miss Thomson adjusted her spectacles and frowned. "However, you are far behind other students your age in many subjects. If you work hard, I'm sure you won't stay in the primary for long." Miss Thomson turned away to give the older children their assignment.

The little girl beside Meg held up her reader and pointed to the list of spelling words. Meg frowned, but she copied the words out on a slate.

The morning passed slowly. After reading, they did sums and geography. Meg, used to walking the streets outside all day, found the small room close and stuffy. She tried hard not to fidget. For noon, Meg and Freddie had brought a hearty lunch of cold chicken, apples and fresh gingerbread. Meg didn't join the children in a game of tag, and when Sally suggested another walk around the playground, she refused. These children, even Sally, seemed so young -- younger even than Mole. She turned away from them and went back inside.

Miss Thomson sat at her desk, marking papers. She looked up as Meg came in.

"Please, Miss Thomson, can I look at your books?" Meg asked.

"May I," Miss Thomson corrected. "Of course. You might try this one first. It's by Walt Whitman." She took a volume bound in red cloth off the shelf. "Study hard, and you'll move forward rapidly." She handed Meg the book and went back to her papers.

Meg nodded her thanks. "Leaves of Grass," and "Edn 1867" shone in gold lettering on the black leather spine. The crisp new pages crackled as Meg opened the book and began reading.

She would have liked to spend the afternoon alone with the books, but after lunch, the class studied history and handwriting. The drone of the children reciting their lessons made her so drowsy she felt her head bobbing.

It seemed forever until Miss Thomson dismissed them for the afternoon. Meg thought of Mole waiting for her, fretting all day. He would have missed her dreadfully. She hurried ahead of Freddie all the way.

But when she got to the stone house in the clearing, Mole was playing marbles with Johnny and barely glanced up at her. So Meg didn't tell him about her day at school. Then Freddie came in, and the two boys set right to work filling the wood box.

Anna handed her a bowl of cornbread batter to finish mixing. "How was school?"

"Fine." Meg's throat felt so tight it was hard to squeeze the word out.

"Michael missed you." Anna wiped Robert's face with her apron corner. "He asked every few minutes when you would be back."

Meg thumped the wooden spoon in the cornbread batter. It sure didn't seem like he missed her any. But it was just as well. If he didn't miss her, he wouldn't hang on her in the morning. She scraped the batter into a pan and gave Robert the wooden spoon to lick, instead of saving it for Mole.

When the wood box was full, Anna told Freddie to fetch some

water, and she sent Meg and Mole into the woods for some bittersweet; a vine with bright orange berries that ripened in the fall.

"Gather an armful," Anna said. "We'll brighten up the kitchen with them." She showed them a branch of it that Freddie had brought in the day before, so they would know what it looked like.

They walked silently to the woods. By now, Meg didn't feel like talking about her day anymore, and Mole didn't ask. Meg felt like they were moving in two different worlds, Mole hurrying off to a place she couldn't follow. Or maybe she was the one leaving him behind after all. Whichever it was, the gulf between them seemed too large to cross.

At the edge of the meadow, Mole stopped. "It's dark in there."

"Don't be a baby!" Meg took his hand to drag him forward.

There was a bit of a path to follow at first. About twenty feet into the stand of aspen and birch, the path dwindled under a soft, brown carpet of leaves. The bright autumn sun overhead turned soft as it filtered through hundreds of orange and yellow leaves. There was a hush all around them. Even the songs of the birds seemed muted.

Then a breeze whispered through the branches, sending a shower of gold fluttering to the ground. Mole clung to Meg's hand. Meg shook him off and twirled in the shadowy light. This was a magic place, like those faery circles Da had talked about. Meg lifted up her arms and spun around again.

"Meg, don't leave me," Mole whined.

Meg twirled again and again. "There's nothing to be afraid of."

"Freddie says there are foxes and bears and wolves in there."

"That Freddie!" Meg snorted. "You can't believe everything he says." She took his hand again and led him further into the trees.

Suddenly Mole screamed. Trembling like the leaves overhead, he whirled to bury his face in her skirt.

"What is it?" Meg asked, alarmed.

Mole wouldn't lift his face. He just pointed behind him. Just ahead, a little off to one side, was a tree like nothing Meg had ever seen before. It towered over them, stark white and naked, the bark stripped from its trunk. Ghostly bare branches stretched out like arms.

"It's just a tree." Meg pushed him around.

"It's a ghost." Mole stepped behind Meg to keep her between him and the tree. "A faery tree, like the ones you told me about; like that rowan tree Da had. I don't like it, Meg. Let's go back."

Meg laughed. "But a rowan never hurt Da or anyone else."

"I'm scared of it." Mole took another step back. "Please, Meg? Let's go another way."

Meg sighed, but she followed him to the edge of the forest and found some bittersweet there. Meg cut it and piled into Mole's arms. Too soon, they had plenty for Anna, and it was time to go back. Mole hurried ahead. Meg lingered, unwilling to leave the golden birches and the ghost tree.

"I'll be back," she whispered as she left. "I promise."

For the next two weeks Meg was much too busy for idle walks. Each morning before she left for school, she washed the breakfast dishes and wiped the table.

Mole continued to watch her silently, standing in the doorway until she was out of sight, but at least he didn't hang on her in the morning anymore or beg her to stay with him.

After school, Meg had chores fixing supper, sweeping the house, and mending clothes with Anna. With four boys, it seemed the mending was never done. Anna talked while they worked together, but never expected much answer which was fine with Meg.

Evenings were the hardest, the time she felt most alone. In the evenings, after the supper dishes were cleared, the family gathered together. Sometimes Hugo read to them while Anna mended. Other times, Hugo and Freddie played checkers. Meg surrounded herself with her schoolbooks and tried to shut out all the emptiness inside her.

One evening, Freddie taught Mole how to play checkers. Mole offered to teach Meg too, but she shook her head.

"Go ahead and play with your brother," Hugo said. "It's your turn."

"I've still got work..." Meg protested.

"A little break from work never hurt anyone," Hugo insisted. "Don't shut yourself away from the family. Play a game with him. Your work will wait."

Reluctantly, she watched Mole set up the checker board and listened as he explained how to play. It seemed so pointless, moving the little black and red markers around. She paid little attention to the game and was relieved when Mole beat her, so she could go back to her work. Mole didn't ask her to play again.

On Saturdays, Anna needed her help in the kitchen. One day they were making pies; pumpkin, apple, and mincemeat. Meg diced the apples and the meat for the mincemeat. She cut up pumpkins and peeled the cooked pieces. Her arms ached from mashing the orange pulp into a smooth and creamy mass, like mashed potatoes.

Then Anna showed her how to roll out crusts for the pies. She made it look easy. But Meg's crusts kept sticking to the rolling pin or falling apart as she tried to pick it up and put it in the tin. The harder she tried, the worse it stuck.

"Don't push down so hard in the middle." Anna showed her again how to let the rolling pin glide across the dough.

Biting her lip, Meg smashed the ruined crust together into a ball. She tried to roll out the dough as Anna had done, but the crust tore in half as one part stuck to the table, and the rolling pin picked up the other part

"It's no good!" Meg threw down the rolling pin with a bang. It skittered across the table and clattered to the floor. She slammed her fist into the ball of pie crust dough and swore. "I can't do this. I'll never be able to."

"Such language." Anna clucked, shaking her head. "It's all right." She bent to pick up the rolling pin, then wiped it off on her apron. "You'll learn." Anna patted Meg's hand. "You work so hard at your studies. It is too much all at once."

Hot anger rose, threatening to overwhelm Meg. Suddenly the room was too small. "No, it's not all right," she yelled. She grabbed her shawl off the peg by the door and stamped off outside.

Maybe she didn't want to make pies. Maybe she couldn't ever learn to make pies. And who would even care? The family? That was a laugh. No one in the family needed her. They had Anna to make them all the pies they wanted.

Without thinking of where she was going, Meg headed up the path and didn't stop until she was beside the ghost tree. It stood silent and bare in the clearing. Meg leaned against the hard, smooth surface of the trunk. Maybe it wasn't a rowan tree like Da talked about, but it was special anyway. Ugly white in the middle of all the golden birches, it didn't pretend everything was all right. It just stood, even after it was dead, tall, alone, unbending.

When Meg went back inside an hour later, the pie crusts were all rolled out and half of them were filled. Meg hung her shawl on the peg by the door. Without looking at Anna she picked up the knife and sat down to dice more apples.

"I'm sorry," she muttered.

"It doesn't matter." Anna didn't smile, and her voice was tired. Ma would have yelled and called her names. Anna never did that, but her silent disapproval was just as strong.

As fall turned to winter, Meg went to school during the week. After school and Saturdays were filled with chores and the end of the harvest. Hugo had Freddie and Mole help him in the fields, and Anna and Meg spent the day doing the wash. Sundays meant the wagon trip to town, and a quiet time at church. When they all sat down together for the noon meal, everyone was too tired to say much. Hugo thanked the Lord for their good fortune at harvest and for the good family they had.

Meg sniffed. As the fall days grew shorter, she wasn't all that sure that backbreaking work from dawn to dusk was really something to be thankful for. It didn't seem much better than selling apples in the street. At least there she had been her own boss. As for family ... well, maybe Ma had been right about that too. Meg was too selfish to be part of any family.

Each day a few more leaves fell off the trees. Soon, stick-like branches stretched up to the leaden sky. Meg still had her old shawl to keep out the cold, and Anna gave her some mittens and a smaller scarf to tie over her ears for the long walk to and from school. A shimmery layer of frost covered the grass each morning and crunched when Meg and Freddie crossed the clearing. Their footprints left a trail of dark spots behind them.

Mole no longer stood in the doorway watching them until they were out of sight.

One cold afternoon, Meg followed Freddie into the house after school just in time to hear Anna asking Mole to bring in more wood. The stone house used a lot of wood to keep the cook stove going and a fire in the fireplace.

"Yes, Mama." Mole skipped out past Meg.

Meg dropped her school books. Johnny jumped up and picked them up for her.

Anna looked up sharply. "Are you all right?"

Meg ignored both of them and spun around to follow Mole outside. She caught up to him by the wood pile, grabbed his arm and jerked him around to face her. He dropped the wood he had picked up. Meg shook him. "She's not your mama!"

"Don't, Meg." Mole struggled to get free of her grip. "She said I could call her Mama."

Meg squeezed his arm. "Don't you remember your own Ma?" Her throat was so tight, the words came out in a harsh whisper.

Mole shook his head. "Not much." He twisted his mouth and squinted his eyes, as if trying to remember. "Just she had blue hands and an ice wagon ran over her. Please, Meg, you're hurting my arm."

There wasn't much more than that to remember, Meg guessed, not for him anyway. Ma hadn't done much for him. Meg let go of his arm.

Mole rubbed it, then bent to pick up the wood he had dropped. "Don't be mad at me, please, Meg. I won't call her Mama if you say not to."

Meg turned away. Why should she even care? Ma was dead. Their old life was gone; nothing was left of their old family. Why shouldn't he call Anna 'Mama,' if that was what he wanted?

Mole touched her sleeve. "I could call you Mama, if you want."

Meg laughed harshly. "I'm not your Mama. No, you go ahead and call Anna Mama, if you want. I guess it don't really matter." She watched him pick up the rest of the wood. She missed the days when it was just the two of them, together. She put a hand to his shoulder. "Walk with me to the woods, Mole," she said. "Just us two. It's not quite dark yet."

Mole edged away from her, toward the door. "But I got to take this wood in. Mama ... Anna's waiting."

"Forget that Anna," Meg said in a flash of anger. "She never minds about anything."

"I got to go in," Mole repeated. He shrank away from her.

Meg kicked the woodpile. "You never did listen to me. No more now than in New York." Meg pushed the words out to keep her own tears in. "You off and fetching Ma that bottle and all. You know you're nothing but a namby-pamby Mama's boy, with whatever Mama comes your way!"

Mole was crying now, but Meg didn't care, or so she told herself with a toss of the head. She turned away from him. It was no use caring anything about him.

"Wait, Meg. What's the matter? Why are you so mad?" His voice caught.

Meg pressed her lips together and started walking.

"Please, Meg? I'd come with you, but it's so dark in there..." There was a catch in his voice.

Meg wouldn't turn around. Let him beg. If he cared, if he cared about her all, he'd come now. She marched across the clearing towards the woods, never turning until she reached the edge. Only then did she glance back to him.

Mole was gone, inside most likely. In to Anna. Let it be that way then. He'd made his choice.

Meg stomped on into the woods to sit by the ghost tree and brood. But this time its stark, pale branches gave her no comfort. She saw instead Mole's pinched, white face, tears streaming down it. Why should she care if he came with her? He never listened to her. He just hung on her and whined when he needed something, and ignored her the rest of the time.

Meg kicked the tree. "It doesn't matter!" she shouted, but only silence answered her. She wished she could take back the hard words she'd given Mole. She'd never meant to make him cry.

But it was no use. She couldn't take back a thing once it was said. Not her words to Mole. Not her words to Ma. Maybe it was best she leave Mole alone, so she didn't hurt him anymore. She'd never been any good for him anyhow. Ma had known that.

CHAPTER 13: DIDN'T I PROMISE?

The next three days were bitterly cold. Anna kept the little boys inside. By the morning of the fourth day, they were wild. They wiggled on the bench during breakfast so much that Johnny fell off the end. That set them all giggling.

As soon as Hugo went out to milk the cow, Freddie started a game of tag around the table. Anna sat in the rocker with her basket of mending. Meg hurried to clear away the breakfast dishes so she could leave for school. She wanted to return the book she had borrowed from the teacher and get another one before school. She was no longer in the primary grade, but she still hadn't caught up to the other twelve year olds.

Meg picked up the milk pitcher and turned to set it back in the cupboard just as Mole darted around the table after Johnny. Johnny slipped past Meg, only brushing her skirt, but Mole crashed into her leg and tripped. Meg dropped the milk pitcher. The tin pitcher clanged as it hit the floor and rolled under the table. Milk ran all over.

Meg whirled to grab Mole. "You clumsy oaf! You got no call to go smashing into people. Look what you done!" She shook him.

Anna stood and put a restraining hand on Meg's arm. "It's all right." She eased Mole free of Meg's grip, then patted Meg's hand. "It's only a little milk. No harm done."

"What do you mean?" Meg snatched up the pitcher from under

the table. "He made a terrible mess. He shouldn't be running in the house." She shook the pitcher at Mole. "You ought to get strapped."

Anna pulled Mole closer. "No, no. Michael is only a little boy. He meant no harm. We'll clean up the milk."

Meg slammed the pitcher down on the table. She felt like screaming. How could Anna say it was all right? Nothing was all right. Mole never listened to her, and Anna never made him do anything. He had to learn to listen to someone, or he would grow up a hooligan. She frowned at Anna. "You're too soft on him."

Anna put her hand on Meg's shoulder. "A little softness won't hurt him. I'll clean up the mess. You go on to school."

Mole slipped out from Anna's protective hug and touched Meg's hand. "I'm sorry." His eyes were wide and bright with worry.

Meg twisted away from both of them. She grabbed her shawl and her books, then ran out. The door slammed behind her.

"Wait for me." Freddie banged out the door after her, but she didn't even slow down.

During the morning recess, Meg stayed inside to study. When it was time for afternoon recess, Miss Thomson closed her book. "That's enough for now," she said as she shooed Meg outside with a bright smile and a soft command that brooked no argument. "All work and no play makes Jill a dull girl."

Meg leaned against the side wall of the school and watched the other children. Sometimes she spent the recess time talking to Sally, but Sally wasn't at school today. Suddenly there was a commotion on the other side of the building. "Fight, fight," she heard some children shouting. She hurried around the corner to see what was going on.

The children gathered in a circle around a tangle of boys. Meg pushed and elbowed her way into the circle until she was near the front. Two bigger boys had grabbed Freddie. One held him with his arms locked back, while the other boy punched him. Freddie kicked at them wildly, but he couldn't get away.

Meg leaped forward. She kicked the boy holding Freddie in the kneecap and then spun around to punch the other boy in the jaw. "You leave him alone or you answer to me!" Meg swore at them.

The first boy let go of Freddie and stumbled backwards. "I ain't fighting no girl," he said warily.

120

The other boy dropped his fists and rubbed his jaw. "Not me either."

Meg sneered. "Why not? Are you chicken?" Kids out here were stronger than city kids she knew, but they didn't know how to fight. She took Freddie's hand. "If you got nothing better to do than fight little boys, then you ain't worth my time." She spun on her heel and walked away from them, dragging Freddie along with her.

The other children stepped aside, opening up the circle for them to get through.

Behind the school, Meg spun Freddie around to face her.

"Gee thanks," he said before she could say anything. "I thought they were going to kill me."

"What kind of a fool thing did you say to get them so riled?" Meg asked.

"Nothing. I just..." He shrugged

"Never mind." Meg brushed her hands off on her skirt. "Go get cleaned up before recess is over. Then keep your mouth shut and stay away from those boys!"

Freddie grinned and ran off to the pump. As she watched him go, Meg wished Mole was there. He used to smile at her like that. She knew she was being selfish, but she didn't want him to hate her. Maybe it wasn't too late to say she was sorry. She hadn't meant to hurt him that night at the woodpile. She hadn't meant to yell at him this morning. Maybe if she said she was sorry he wouldn't mind so much.

Maybe he'd even smile at her again.

Late that afternoon, Meg walked home slowly, planning what she would say to Mole. First she would invite him outside for a walk, just a short one, not to the woods. She couldn't take back her angry words, but she could say she was sorry. That had to mean something. She never had a chance to say that to Ma. Meg was so busy thinking she never noticed that Freddie ran on ahead.

When Meg stepped inside the stone house, Freddie was busy telling them all how she had saved him at recess. Mole sat on the floor playing marbles with the smaller boys. He didn't turn around as she closed the door.

Anna looked up from her mending and shook her finger at Meg. "Young ladies should not be brawling, and Freddie needs to mind his tongue." With a sigh, she bent her head to continue darning the sock in her lap and went on in a softer voice. "But you have been a good big sister today."

Meg scowled. How could she have been any kind of a good sister to Freddie? Mole was her brother, not Freddie.

Mole hunched over the marbles. He still hadn't looked at her.

Meg put her school books down. "Come for a walk with me, Mole," she said, but the words came out like she was giving an order. She lowered her voice and tried again. "Just to the pasture."

Mole kept his back to her. "It's awful cold outside," he said.

"We won't go to the woods."

Mole curled in smaller and didn't answer.

Meg stared at him helplessly. The silence between them grew. Meg couldn't apologize in here, not with everyone listening. Freddie crunched noisily into an apple at the table. Robert scooped up all the marbles in front of him and divided them out with Johnny. Anna stirred the stew and added another stick of wood to the fire. No one was paying any attention to Meg, standing there, or Mole, with his back to her. But Meg couldn't say the words in here.

"Freddie, Michael, the woodbox," Anna reminded them.

"I'll get it." Mole grabbed his coat. He edged out the door, not looking at Meg.

She followed him out. "Mole?" She touched his shoulder.

He jerked away as if she had hit him.

"What's wrong?" she asked.

He bent over the woodpile, picking out sticks he could carry. "Nothing." There was a catch in his voice as he straightened and sidled toward the door with his armful of split logs. Passing her, he glanced back. His eyes were shiny in the fading light.

"You're crying, Mole," Meg said in surprise. "What's wrong? I never said anything this time."

"My name's Michael!" He lifted his shoulder to smear away the tear on his cheek. "But I don't guess you'd care. If it was bullies after me at school, you'd never be saving me. If it was bullies after me, you'd just be yelling at me." His voice shook as he glared at her. Then he

122

dropped his gaze and shuffled toward the house.

Meg grabbed his elbow. "Wait, Mole..."

He shook free of her and pushed inside, kicking the door shut behind him.

Meg stared at the planks of the closed door for a long time. She had wanted to say she was sorry, but he never gave her a chance. What did he mean about his name? She had always called him Mole. Why did he want something else now? Everything was Anna's fault, putting ideas in his head, taking him away from her.

A cold wind swirled the leaves around the woodpile. Meg pulled her shawl tighter and felt the soft, frayed edge against her cheek. But instead of giving her any warmth, the wool only made her think of Ma.

Turning her back on the stone house and everyone in it, she ran all the way to the ghost tree in the woods. There in the silence of the birch woods, she kicked the tree and called Mole an ungrateful little beggar. Her words were loud in the empty woods. Their echo sounded hollow, like the hole in the pit of her stomach. She kicked the tree again and again.

Finally, she collapsed beside the tree, her cheek pressed against the cold, smooth bark. Overhead a great V of geese honked raucously as they flew past, heading somewhere else.

Meg realized she ought to leave too. No one here would miss her; not Hugo, or Anna, not the boys and certainly not Mole. He had learned how selfish she was, just like Ma knew. What a fool she'd been to wish for any of this.

Meg rubbed her shoulders and stamped her feet to get the chill out. It was no use fussing over that now. She didn't belong here. She would just have to forget about Mole, seeing as he didn't want any part of her. Meg shoved her hands deep into her skirt pockets. It would be best for everyone if she just left.

That night, Meg stood for a long time at the attic window. She stared though the lace curtains toward the woods surrounding the clearing. The moon was full in a clear sky. White snow shone softly in gentle mounds and humps. Once she had thought lace curtains at the window would be enough.

Mole crept up beside her. He stuck his hand in hers. Startled, Meg looked down at him. His face was filling out from the good food here, so he didn't look so rat-like anymore. Suddenly, Meg wanted to clutch him to her and hug so tight she would never have to let go. Of course, he'd never let her do that. She let go of his hand and turned back to the window.

"You're fixing to leave, ain't you?" he said.

"What makes you say that?" Meg kept her voice steady.

Mole shrugged. "You are, ain't you?"

"Maybe. What difference does it make?"

"Don't leave me here, Meg." His voice was urgent. "Take me with you when you go."

Meg turned to look at him. "But you like it here. You've got Hugo and Anna and Freddie and the rest. It's a good place for you."

Mole shook his head hard. "Not without you. Promise you won't leave me behind."

"I thought you were mad at me." Meg felt strangely warmed by the thought he wanted to be with her.

"I'm not mad anymore. Promise me."

Meg ruffled his hair. She had taken care of him all his life, and now she had found a good home for him. It was plain selfish to want to keep him with her. Ma would be proud of her at last. She would leave him here, where he belonged. She wouldn't hurt him anymore. He would get over missing her, just like he got over Ma. She squeezed his hand. "Oh, Moley, didn't I promise you that a long time ago?"

"Do it again," he insisted.

"Oh, all right. I promise."

Mole reached up and hugged her, then scampered off to bed.

Meg stared after him. She had never lied to him before.

CHAPTER 14: LUCKY ENOUGH

Meg beat the cornbread batter with the wooden spoon. Mole knelt on the bench and leaned his elbows on the table.

"Shove over. Let me finish mixing it." Meg poured the batter into the greased tin pan. She liked having Mole beside her, but she couldn't let him get too used to it; not if she wanted to do what was best for him. She set the pan in the oven on the side of the cookstove.

"I get the first lick!" Freddie wormed his way in between Mole and Meg.

"Not hardly." Mole pushed Freddie. "I was here first."

Freddie shoved him back.

"You two hush your yammering, or you won't either one of you get a lick." Meg set the bowl down on the table. "Now you share that with Johnny," she ordered. She handed Robert the spoon to lick and set him up to the table. While the boys squabbled over the bowl, she set about frying some salt pork.

The cornbread was just finished baking when Hugo came in, stomping fresh snow off his feet and shaking it from his shoulders. "The snow is letting up, at least for a bit. After breakfast we will cut a Christmas tree."

Meg set the pitcher of buttermilk on the table. Christmas. She hadn't had Christmas since Da died.

"You mean those prickly trees they used to sell in New York?

What do we need a Christmas tree for?" Mole asked.

Freddie gaped at him. "Don't you know nothing?"

Hugo laughed, picked Mole up and swung him in the air before he and Freddie could squabble. "It's a custom from the old country. We'll pick out the prettiest pine tree for miles around, cut it down, and bring it inside the house to decorate."

"And there will be presents on it," Freddie said.

"And popcorn," Johnny remembered.

"And Mama has three silver balls to hang on it," Freddie added.

"And candles," Johnny said, his eyes shining.

Hugo laughed again. "This year Freddie and Michael can come along to help pick out the prettiest tree and cut it down." He sat down at the head of the table. "But first we'll eat this delicious breakfast your sister has cooked."

Meg set the plate of steaming cornbread on the table. Anna came into the kitchen.

"Papa says we get to cut a Christmas tree today." Freddie jumped up and down eagerly.

Anna smiled. "Ja, but you must eat first." She pulled him down beside her. "This breakfast smells delicious, Meg."

After they had eaten, Anna helped Freddie bundle up in his warmest clothes. Then she turned to Mole and held out his jacket.

Mole held back. "Are we going to the woods for a Christmas tree?"

Meg helped herself to a piece of cornbread. "Don't be silly, Mole. Where else would you find a tree?"

"We won't go in far," Hugo said. "Just a little ways."

Mole shook his head. "I don't want to go. I want to stay inside with Meg." He squeezed up beside her at the table, bumping her arm and making her slop buttermilk onto her plate.

"Go on, Mole." She shoved him away. "Don't be a scaredy-cat."

"No. I don't want to go in the woods." He was almost crying.

"It's all right," Anna said. "Maybe Michael can go next year." She sat in the rocker and patted her lap.

Mole looked at Meg, then climbed down from the table and into Anna's lap.

"You can't keep running away from the things you're scared

of," Meg said to him. She got a rag to wipe the buttermilk up.

Mole didn't answer. Anna slowly rocked him. "He won't," she said softly.

Hugo and Freddie went out without him. Meg swiped at the buttermilk. It didn't matter that she had lied to him. He never did listen to her. Not ever.

Meg finished her breakfast and started washing the dishes. It was quiet in the kitchen. The fire in the hearth crackled. Robert and Johnny knelt on the bench under the front window, drawing pictures in the frost and watching for Hugo and Freddie.

Before long, Mole climbed down from Anna's lap to come stand by Meg. Silently, he watched her swish the dishrag in the dishpan and wipe the tin plate clean. Then he touched her sleeve. "You want some help with that?" he asked.

"No," Meg said crossly. "You'd just get water all over the place."

"You can help me wind this yarn, Michael," Anna said. Mole looked once more at Meg, then sat on the floor in front of Anna and held up his hands for her to wind the new yarn on.

Meg sighed. Anna was always there, and Mole always went to her. He wouldn't care at all when she left, not the least bit. Oh, he might whine a little, but Anna would comfort him. He would forget about her in no time, and she had best forget about him too. But it was no good leaving before the snow melted and spring came, she reminded herself. It was a long walk to town.

She wished Danny hadn't stolen Jake's watch from her. She would have been able to go a long way selling that. Maybe she could get a job in town, in a house or store. She had learned a lot of cooking and cleaning. Meg swished the dishrag in the soapy water. After she got a job, she'd save up her money and buy a train ticket back to New York. It wouldn't be so bad there now. Jake would never find her in that mass of people. Without Mole to worry about, she could get along just fine. She didn't need Anna or Mole or any of them.

That thought reminded her uncomfortably of Danny. He hadn't needed anyone either. She shook her head to clear away the memory. She wasn't going to be like Danny, stealing from little kids. She just needed to worry about her own self now, and that was all.

It started snowing early on Christmas eve, a light, powdery snow that sparkled in the lantern light. There was to be a program at the school house. Hugo hitched up the team, and they piled into the wagon after supper.

The air was crisp. The horses' breath came out in steaming clouds, and the snow squeaked beneath their hooves. Anna sat on the wagon seat next to Hugo, with Robert wrapped up in her lap. Meg and the other three boys were bundled together in the back. They shared the heavy wool blankets and squeezed close together for warmth, but Meg felt herself far away from the others.

When Freddie started singing one of the Christmas carols they had learned at school, first Hugo and then Anna joined in. After the first round, Mole joined in on the chorus. His voice was just a little off key, but it was sweet. Meg, listening quietly to the others, realized she had never heard him sing before.

After the service, the folk gathered in bunches to catch up with each other. Most of the neighbors lived far enough out of town that Sundays were the only day they had for visiting. It was too cold to go outside, so the children played tag or hide and seek around the clusters of adults. Anna and three or four others talked about the best way to keep bugs out of the flour. Hugo and the men were all talking of the harvest.

Meg stood apart from the others, in a corner by the door. She could join Sally with the girls from school. They would let her in, she knew. No one had been unfriendly, but she didn't feel like talking. She wished things were different, but in the end she was not like all the people here. In New York, no one expected anything from her. No one even knew her. Perhaps it meant no one noticed when she was gone, but it also meant she never disappointed anyone either.

Her melancholy thoughts were interrupted by a commotion on the other side of the room. A big man, even bigger than Hugo, had Mole by the collar and was shaking him.

Meg dashed across the room, elbowing aside anyone in her way. "Leave go of him," she yelled. She had just enough time to aim a kick at his shin, before Hugo grabbed her arm and jerked her back.

"What is the problem?" Hugo kept a tight hold on her.

"This young scalawag from New York is a thief!" the big man spluttered. "He's taken my watch." He had Mole's shirt twisted up in his right hand. He held the boy so his toe tips barely touched the floor, and he punctuated each word with shake.

Mole squirmed and twisted to get away.

Hugo let go of Meg and took hold of the man's wrist to stop him. "Calm down, Karl. He is also my son," he said quietly. "I will deal with him."

Karl let go of Mole, who ducked behind Hugo the minute he was released. Hugo placed a hand on the boy's shoulder and pulled him forward.

Mole thrust his hands deep in his pockets and kept his eyes on Hugo's shoes.

"What about my watch? The little beggar has it in his pocket."

"Michael? Is that true?" Hugo asked.

Slowly Mole took his hand out of his pocket and uncurled his fingers from around the watch.

Hugo picked it up out of his hand. The expression on his face was grim as he handed the watch back to Karl. "I'm sorry."

Anna had come up and joined the circle around them. Her boys, silent for once, clustered around her, and her eyes looked tired.

"What is this about?" Hugo asked Mole.

Mole looked up, first at Hugo, than at Anna, then at Meg. He stared at her a long time, his eyes pleading.

With a sickening jolt, Meg thought he was going to tell. She'd be sent back, not free to pick up her own life, but to prison, to Blackwell's, to a dark, cold cell.

But Mole wasn't saying anything. He gave a little shrug of his bony shoulders and sagged as if defeated. Everyone was staring at him now, and on each face Meg saw a reflection of everyone who had ever scowled at her for being poor, everyone who had ever kicked her out of the way when she was scrounging for food. It wasn't fair. He was just a little boy.

"It's not his fault." She broke the silence in the crowded room. "It's my fault." She rushed to get the words out before the eyes, staring at her now, numbed her back into silence. "I stole a watch first. He's just copying me." She turned to Mole and spoke to him as if he were the only one in the room. "Why did you do it, Moley? Why did you take his watch now?" All he'd ever taken before was food.

Mole twisted the toe of his boot into the floor. His eyes darted around the room, searching every face but hers. For help? For some sort of escape? She thought he wasn't going to answer her. But he must not have found what he was looking for, because finally, still without looking at her, he whispered, "To help you out, Meg. I knew you missed that watch something awful. I done it for you."

His words echoed in the silent room as if he had shouted them.

"What happened?" Hugo asked. "What is this watch you say you stole? And where is it now?"

Meg looked down at the floor. "He's talking about Jake's watch."

"Who is Jake?" Hugo prodded.

She hesitated. How could she explain Jake? Not her stepfather, for sure. But she couldn't bring herself to call Jake Ma's boyfriend. "He lived with us before Ma died." Meg shrugged. "We stayed on with him afterwards. I took the watch when he kicked us out. I guess I figured he owed us something. But he came after us, looking for it."

With gentle coaxing from Hugo, bit by bit the whole story of how she took Jake's watch, and how Danny had stolen it away from her spilled out. Even though she knew everyone was listening, Meg told it to the Steins. She owed them that, she guessed. But at the end she turned to Karl, the man who had caught Mole. "I'm awful sorry, Mister. I never meant to teach him stealing."

"I'm sorry, too," Mole added.

Karl frowned. "I hate to see thieving go unpunished."

"I think it has not," Hugo said slowly. "The burden of the first watch has been with this young lady for a long time, even after she no longer had it. "

"Well," Karl said. "It is Christmas Eve, and I trust you know what's best in your own family. There's no real harm done, I suppose." He shook Hugo's hand.

The ride home in the wagon was very quiet, with none of the singing they had shared on the way in. No one said a word as they left the town behind. The night was still, and the little boys soon fell asleep. Meg was reminded of her first ride out, when she was so worried about Mole. Everything had changed since then. A place to sleep, enough

130

food, the things she had worried so much over before didn't seem to be enough anymore. Mole needed more than a place to sleep; he needed a place to call his home, a place to grow up right. A place like the Stein's home. How could she find him a place like this if they had to go back to New York?

The others were all asleep when Hugo drove into the yard. Anna carried Robert in. Hugo shook Freddie and Mole awake. They stumbled after her.

Before Hugo picked up Johnny, Meg grabbed his arm. As much as she was afraid of the answer, she had to know the worst. "Please…" She swallowed and tried again. "Please. Are you going to send us back now? Mole … Michael … he's not a bad boy. He didn't know…" Meg took a deep breath, and tried to keep her voice steady. "You can send me back if you have to. I…I can get by anywhere, but Mole … Michael, please keep him. He needs you."

"You need each other." Hugo frowned. "But no one is going to be sent back."

"You're not sending us back?" Meg's eyes widened in surprise. A wave of relief washed over her; so strong she had to grab the edge of the wagon to steady herself. Mole would be safe.

Hugo rested his hand on her shoulder. "You have disappointed Anna and me. But we made a promise to you, and you to us, to be a family, and so we are a family now. Families take care of each other. You have to believe that." He squeezed gently, then turned away from her to pick up Johnny and walk inside.

Meg followed him. She should have felt glad. At least Mole could keep the family he needed. But her heart was just as heavy as it had been all evening. She was the one ruining this family, but they kept showing her kindness. It might have been easier if Hugo had decided to send her back.

In spite of the late night, the children all woke up early on Christmas morning. There were presents, just as Freddie had said there would be. For each of the boys Anna had knitted a warm scarf and a matching pair of mittens. They each got a sack of new marbles and a long, red and white peppermint stick.

Mole's whole face lit up when he tasted it. "This is good!" He licked it slowly and carefully to make it last all day. For Meg there was a beautiful green shawl. She touched it with her fingertips. It was so soft, softer even than the frayed edge of her old, brown shawl. It was much warmer.

"It's just the right shade of green to match your eyes." Hugo nodded approvingly. "Try it on."

Meg unfolded the shawl to put it over her shoulders. She didn't say a word, not even thank you. She couldn't. They shouldn't have given her presents. She didn't deserve anything. She bent her head so the soft fringe brushed her cheek.

Soon Hugo went out to feed and water the animals, taking Mole and Freddie with him. When Mole came inside later, he had a present for Anna. "I made it myself." He handed her a pine branch twisted in a circle and decorated with dried bittersweet berries. "It isn't very good. I hope you like it."

Meg snorted. The bundle looked a lot like the things he used to call cockroach traps made out of sticks and pieces of dirty string.

"I didn't have much time," Mole was saying. "I didn't know anything about Christmas. Freddie told me about wreaths and things. Maybe, if you like it, you could hang it on the door."

Anna's eyes glistened. "It is beautiful, Michael. Just beautiful." She dabbed her apron against her eyes. "Of course I will hang it on the door." She pulled him close and kissed the top of his head.

Meg turned her face away. She picked up a walnut and put it in the nutcracker. She turned the handle until the nut broke with a loud and satisfying crack. Slowly she picked out the nut meat and then smashed another. There was a family here, all right, just as Hugo had said the night before. But she wasn't a part of it.

Hugo got out his hammer and a nail. He pushed the bench from the table over by the door and stood Mole up on it. With a little help, Mole pounded in the nail and hung his wreath on it.

Then Mole sat beside Meg at the table. For awhile he watched her without saying anything. He handed her a nut. She cracked it and gave the nut meat to him.

"I would have made a present for you too, Meg," he said softly. "But I couldn't make it come out right. I figured you'd be mad if it didn't come out right." He stared at her for a minute. She went on cracking nuts and picking out the meats, without saying a word. "You ain't mad, are you?" he asked, touching her hand.

She shook free of him. He had tried to get her a present, the kind of present he thought she'd want--a stolen watch. "Course I ain't mad. What's to be mad about?"

"You look awful mad."

"Well, I ain't, so quit bothering me." Meg felt as if her heart would break. She couldn't face him, not if she wanted to stay strong enough to leave.

Mole blinked twice, then slid off the bench away from her.

After dinner the boys played marbles on the floor. Hugo got out his harmonica. Meg washed the dishes and sat by the fire, staring at the flames flickering quietly on the hearth. As she sat, the cozy kitchen grew hotter and hotter, until Meg felt like she was suffocating. The boys played without squabbling. Anna hummed along with the harmonica as she knit. Hugo's music was bright and cheery.

Meg thought she was going to scream. She jumped up and grabbed her new shawl as she dashed outside, away from the quiet happiness, the overwhelming peace and kindness. She didn't pay any attention to Mole, who put down his marbles as he watched her leave.

It was very cold outside, the kind of cold that burned her cheeks and ears. She pulled the new shawl tightly around her shoulders, but gave up the idea of walking to the woods and seeing the ghost tree. Instead, she went to the barn. It was warmer in there, and the horse and the cow didn't worry about who belonged anywhere.

"You're not so scary," she said to Lotte. Then she felt foolish for talking to a cow. What did the cow know about scaring anyone? All it cared about was food and a warm place to stay. A cow never cried because it had to leave. A cow couldn't be bothered with that kind of foolishness.

Cows weren't much good as company either. Unlike the ghost tree, silent and unmoving, a cow kept reminding you it was there. Lotte shifted about and rustled in the stall, munching on its feed. Most of all, a cow looked at you, with soft, sad eyes. Meg didn't want to think about cows being sad. She climbed to the hayloft where Lotte couldn't look at her.

There were no windows in the loft, leaving it dim and gloomy. The piled hay was itchy. Bits of straw poked through her apron and skirt. As soon as she settled herself, she started sneezing. She stood up and kicked the hay. There was nothing to do, nowhere to go, nowhere to be alone.

Outside the barn she thought once more about walking to the woods, but it was already starting to get dark. Heavy grey clouds pushed in from the west warning that more snow was on the way. She went inside.

Anna looked up from the sideboard where she was carving the leftover turkey for supper. "Tell Michael to come in too. It's getting late, and we'll eat supper soon."

"He wasn't with me," Meg said.

Anna stopped, her knife hovering over the turkey platter. "He went out right after you did."

Hugo set his harmonica down. "Don't worry, Anna. I'll go find him. Likely he's out in the barn visiting Lotte." He threw on his jacket and went out.

Meg knew he wasn't in the barn since she had just been in there. She pulled her shawl back on. "I'll go too." She hurried out before Anna could protest.

Hugo was already halfway across the yard to the barn. Meg didn't follow him. She stood outside the door. If Mole wasn't in the barn, where could he be? Maybe he had gone down to the pasture. Meg started across the yard. She couldn't imagine why he would go to the pasture. It was too cold for playing outside. He never went to the creek without Freddie. If he was just hiding, playing a joke on them, she'd see he got whipped for it, no matter what Anna said.

Halfway across the yard, Meg noticed small boot tracks in the snow, heading towards the woods.

She stopped. They couldn't be Mole's. He would never go to the woods. But none of the other boys had been out.

With a sinking feeling, Meg turned to follow the tracks. The cold was bitter. Meg's toes and fingers tingled. If Mole was in the woods, he'd be nearly frozen by now. She started to run, but then she stopped. If ever she needed to do right by Mole, it was now. She didn't need to do this alone. "Families help each other," Hugo had said. If

Mole was out in the woods, he would need more than just her.

She ran back toward the barn. "Hugo," she called. "This way!"

Hugo came at once. Together they followed the small boot tracks around the house and up to the woods behind it, along the path she took to the ghost tree. They hurried, neither one speaking of the fear both knew.

Meg felt a sick churning in her stomach, like she'd had the night Da went away, like she'd had when she saw Ma lying in the street. She always made everything go wrong. A wave of nausea gripped her, but she hurried on, running a bit to keep up with Hugo's longer strides.

Once they were inside the shelter of the trees, the wind was quieter. The snow wasn't so deep. There was an intense stillness in the air, as if everything in the woods held its breath, waiting.

Hugo and Meg came to a rocky spot, and the tracks ended.

"Mole?" Meg called. Only the wind sighing in the trees answered her. "Mole!" she screamed. "Where are you?"

Hugo pointed to the right. "You go that way. Circle the woods and meet on the far side, by the north pasture. I'll go this way." He stomped off to the left without waiting for her answer.

Overhead, a bare branch rattled. Meg jumped. What did Mole have to go and run off for anyhow? She kicked at the snow, sending up a cloud of white, icy powder. He was nothing but a pack of trouble, that's all.

A big black crow cawed in complaint and flapped away. Meg shook herself. She didn't want to be angry anymore. Not with Mole. Not with anyone. There had been so much anger. Da had died with Ma angry. Ma had died while Meg was angry. If anything happened to Mole now, Meg thought she couldn't stand it. It wasn't wealth she needed; it wasn't the watch to get her back to New York. It wasn't even being alone, without worrying over Mole anymore. She couldn't ever stop worrying about him, no matter how far away she went. What she needed, all she needed, was her brother. What she needed was Mole.

"Mole," she screamed again, but this time her voice came out as a sob.

She shivered. She couldn't think this way. She just had to find him. She came to the ghost tree. There was no sign of him, only bare trees and piles of brambles.

Hesitantly, Meg reached out and touched the tree's cold white trunk. For luck, if there was any. For Da and Ma and the rowan tree. She closed her eyes. "Mole," she whispered. "Where are you?"

Suddenly, a cold, wet child hurled himself at her, knocking them both down.

"Meg," he sobbed. "You came back."

Meg sat in the snow and hugged him to her so tightly it hurt. She wouldn't let him go, not ever. With her arms wrapped around him, she rocked back and forth while he cried.

Finally, she lifted up his face and brushed away his tears with the fringe of her shawl. "What are you doing out here?" she scolded, but her voice was gentle, not the sharp voice she had used with him so often. "You'll be making yourself sick all over again."

Mole's teeth chattered. "I thought you left without me. I went after you, but I couldn't catch up to you." He sobbed again and buried his face in her shoulder. "I thought you was gone for good. Without me." His words were so choked Meg could barely understand them. "Don't be mad at me, Meg, please."

Meg rocked him back and forth. "But you're scared of the woods." She didn't wipe away the tears rolling down her own cheeks now. Her voice broke. "You came after me even in the woods?"

Mole gulped and nodded. "I thought you was gone," he said again as if that explained everything.

With a deep, shuddering breath, Meg clutched him to her. Then she took off her new shawl and wrapped it around him. "We've got to get you back inside. You're nearly frozen." He was too big for her to carry, and he was shivering too much to walk now. She needed help.

"Hugo," she screamed. "I've found him." She called again and again, until she heard the crunching in the brush that meant Hugo was on the way.

As she called, she thought about Mole running off to the woods to find her. No matter how scared he was, he'd come after her. Maybe he did need her as much as she needed him. Maybe Hugo was right.

"P-please don't leave me, Meg." Mole's teeth chattered so hard he could barely talk. "P-please take me with you."

Meg wrapped her arms around him again. All this time, he had been wanting her, needing her, and she had kept running from him, pushing him away from her. She shook her head. Not anymore. She couldn't get by in New York without him. She couldn't get by anywhere without him. She saw that now. Ma had shriveled up and died inside when Da left. She could have loved them, could have kept the family she still had, but she hadn't been able to. Meg wouldn't make the same mistake.

"Oh, Moley, we're a couple of fools sitting out here in the snow, letting the tears freeze on our cheeks." She tried to laugh, but it came out more like a sob.

Hugo strode into the clearing and wrapped his arms around them both. "Thank the Lord."

Meg stood up, pulling Mole to his feet too. "I'm all through running." She looked straight into his eyes. "I won't ever leave you. Never. I promise."

"You really mean that?" Mole asked with a tremor in his voice.

Meg nodded. "We're a family now. Families help each other."

That's what everyone had been saying all along. Ma, when she didn't want Da to leave, and Da when he tried to help his friends. Now Hugo and Anna, who never gave up on her.

Hugo scooped Mole up into his arms and winked at her. "You mind your sister, Michael. She knows what's good for you."

"I guess I'm lucky you found me," Mole said.

She took his hand, and matched her steps to Hugo's as they left the woods. Anna would be inside the house, with a warm fire going, and a smile for them both. It would be enough.

"I guess we're both lucky," Meg said. "Let's go home, Michael."

BEHIND THE STORY

Meg and her brother, Mole, are fictional characters, but the slum they lived in and the so-called 'orphan train' they took west are both very real.

Jacob Riis, a photographer and journalist from second half of the 19th century studied the terrible living conditions in the slums and tenements of New York City. Using his own photographs, along with the photographs of others, he published a book in 1890, called *How the Other Half Lives: Studies Among the Tenements of New York*. This book presents the grim reality of the life for the very poor. The book served as a model for describing the tenement that Meg and Mole inhabit with their mother at the beginning of their story.

Meg and Mole escape their life of poverty by going west on an orphan train. The true story of these orphan trains began with a young minister named Charles Loring Brace. When he came to New York, he saw thousands of children with no home and no one to care for them. Some people estimate that there were at least 30,000 orphans living on the streets. These children slept in alleys or doorways, or over heating grates if they could find them. They earned a living by selling rags, matches, papers, flowers or apples. Many of them turned to begging or stealing to stay alive. A great many of them did not survive.

The streets of New York were filled with so many homeless children partly because of the huge numbers of people moving into the city to work in the factories. Immigrants from Ireland and other parts of Europe filled the city, hoping to escape famine and poverty in their home countries. Desperately poor, these families crowded together in some of the worst slums in the Five Points District of New York City. Disease and crime tore families apart.

The Civil War also contributed to the number of orphans left homeless in the city. Thousands of men had died in Civil War. Their widows were often too poor to take care of their children. And, like Meg and Mole's father, at least 120 civilians died during the week of Draft Riots in July of 1863. These riots started as a protest for the newly instituted draft. Most of the rioters were Irish immigrants. They were angry at being forced into the army and by the fact that wealthier men could pay a fee to hire a substitute. Although these riots started as a protest against the draft, the riot turned into a racial attack against the Black poplutaion of New York.

With so many homeless children in need, Mr. Brace came up with a plan to help. He had already founded the Children's Aid Society in 1852, with the mission of locating good homes for poor orphans. Mr. Brace believed that orphanages were not the best place for such children. He worried that the children did not receive enough training for life in orphanages. He was convinced that orphans would thrive in good country homes where the air was fresh, and there was plenty of good food and wholesome work. He said, "The best of all asylums for the outcast child is the farmer's home."[1] So he set about trying to find this kind of home for all of New York's orphans.

When the Children's Aid Society opened its doors, hundreds of children applied for help. Also, farmers around New York were eager for an extra pair of hands and were willing to offer their homes to a child. In fact, the response to Mr. Brace's plan was so great that Mr. Brace soon realized placing out the children one at a time was much too slow. So, he organized companies of children to send to towns all over New York and out to the Midwest. The first such train left New York in 1854, carrying 46 children to new homes.

According to the plan, each child received room, board and an education in return for the child's labor. Younger children were usually adopted by the family that took them in and older children might be paid for their work. This idea of placing out or fostering orphans had been popular in America since colonial times, but Mr. Brace was the first to try to find homes for children on such a large and systematic scale.

Before each company left New York City, the Children's Aid Society contacted several towns. When the group of children arrived, a committee made up of local citizen helped the Society agents decide on each of the applications to adopt or employ a child. Any child who didn't find a home in the first town went on to the next.

Most of the children who were sent west were indeed orphans, but some had one or both parents still living. For many reasons, these parents were unable to care for their children. They gave the Children's Aid Society permission to place their children with a new family in the

West. In many cases, the Children's Aid Society helped the children and parents keep in touch with each other. Sometimes a fostered child was even able to help the rest of the family move west, escaping the slums of New York.

The system worked well for many children, but not for all. Some families who employed an orphan treated that child cruelly. Some of the children couldn't get used to the difference between city life and country life. Another problem was that not everyone agreed with Mr. Brace's system. They worried the children sent west would lose their religion or would be mistreated. Others worried that the children would cause more crime and other problems in the towns they came to.

In order to address these questions, the Children's Aid Society agreed to check on the children on a regular basis. Mr. Brace published yearly reports on the children, along with many of their letters. Some of these letters helped me imagine Meg and Mole's journey and their life with the Stein family. Mr. Brace's system was not perfect, but it gave many children a new chance at life.

Eventually the Children's Aid Society decided it was better for the homeless children to be placed in foster care near New York City, where they could remain closer to any relatives still living. Many new agencies began helping families stay together, and other agencies worked to improve sanitation and health in the slums.

With these advances in social welfare, the orphan trains were no longer necessary. The last orphan train ran in 1929. One young man, John G. B., left New York in 1859 on an orphan train. Years later, in 1871, after he graduated from college and became a successful teacher, John wrote, "To be taken from the gutters of New York and placed in a college is almost a miracle."[2] Even after being taken into Hugo and Anna Stein's home, adjusting to this new life wasn't easy for Meg Kelly. But in the end, I think she would agree with John.

[1] Brace, Charles Loring. *The Dangerous classes of New York and twenty years' work among them.* Wynkoop and Hollenbeck, 1872.

[2] Brady, John Green. from a letter quoted by Brace in *The Dangerous classes of New York and twenty years' work among them.* (see above)
John G. Brady later became governor of Alaska.

Terri Karsten

ABOUT THE AUTHOR

Ever since she was a little girl, reading books about Caddie Woodlawn and Laura Ingalls Wilder, Terri Karsten has loved imagining what life was like for children long ago. To make her stories as accurate as possible, she has gone beyond reading to practising living history. She has travelled by wagon train in the Dakotas and by steam train in Minnesota, and she has cooked countless pioneer meals over a campfire in Rendezvous reenactments.

Currently Ms. Karsten lives with her husband in a hundred year old house near the Mississippi River. She enjoys travelling, playing with her grandchildren, and hiking the beautiful bluffs near her home when she isn't reading or writing.

Look for other books by Terri Karsten at terrikarsten.com

Made in the USA
Monee, IL
23 February 2023

28007873R00090